"Who could possibly have ~~...~~ **old country lawyer?"**

. . . Asked Cynthia Shays-Trask.

"Now, I never said anything about murder." Sheriff Armstrong said.

"So he died from heart failure. He's still dead, isn't he?"

Armstrong said, "No, as a matter of fact it *was* murder, but I'm curious to know why you jumped to that conclusion."

"Sheriff, I live in a large city. When I hear someone has died my mind naturally jumps to murder."

Ashley Trask-Cooper asked, "Sheriff, what exactly does this have to do with us?"

"That's what I was hoping you'd be able to tell me. The safe in his office was standing wide open, but as far as his secretary can tell, there's only one thing missing. She found an empty folder with the heading, 'THE LAST WILL AND TESTAMENT OF MATHIAS TRASK' on it."

At that moment, Cynthia Shays-Trask fainted dead away.

A LIGHTHOUSE INN MYSTERY

"Book me at Hatteras West any day!"
—Tamar Myers, author of *Gruel and Unusual Punishment*

Lighthouse Inn Mysteries by Tim Myers

INNKEEPING WITH MURDER
MURDER WITH RESERVATIONS
MURDER CHECKS INN

MURDER
CHECKS INN

Tim Myers

BERKLEY PRIME CRIME, NEW YORK

This is a work of fiction. Names, characters, places, and incidents either are the product of the author's imagination or are used fictitiously, and any resemblance to actual persons, living or dead, business establishments, events, or locales is entirely coincidental.

MURDER CHECKS INN

A Berkley Prime Crime Book / published by arrangement with the author

PRINTING HISTORY
Berkley Prime Crime mass-market edition / January 2003

Copyright © 2003 by Tim Myers.
Cover art by Yuan Lee.
Cover design by Jill Boltin.
Text design by Kristin del Rosario.

All rights reserved.
This book, or parts thereof, may not be reproduced in any form without permission.
For information address: The Berkley Publishing Group,
a division of Penguin Putnam Inc.,
375 Hudson Street, New York, New York 10014.

Visit our website at
www.penguinputnam.com

ISBN: 0-425-18858-2

Berkley Prime Crime Books are published
by The Berkley Publishing Group,
a division of Penguin Putnam Inc.,
375 Hudson Street, New York, New York 10014.
The name BERKLEY PRIME CRIME and
the BERKLEY PRIME CRIME design
are trademarks belonging to Penguin Putnam Inc.

PRINTED IN THE UNITED STATES OF AMERICA

10 9 8 7 6 5 4 3 2 1

For my mother, Ruby Hall,
and my father, Bob Myers.

For my daughter, Emily,
who believes with all her heart that she's the real reason
I became a writer (and in a way, it's true, Emma).

And, most of all,
for my wife, Patty,
who never lost the faith, even when she had
every reason in the world to.

This one's for you all.

1

"I still don't know why we had to come all the way out to the middle of nowhere to read Father's will," Ashley Trask-Cooper said impatiently, smoothing the invisible wrinkles from her pantsuit with abbreviated flicks of her hand as she spoke. It was readily apparent that Ashley wasn't used to waiting for anyone. She had asked her mother and brother the same question a dozen times since they'd recently arrived. It was obvious the Hatteras West Inn was the last place in the world Ashley wanted to be.

Alex Winston looked up from his position behind the check-in desk at the people who had been fidgeting in the lobby of Hatteras West for the last forty minutes. Though they hadn't introduced themselves upon their arrival, it hadn't been all that difficult for Alex to match names with faces.

When no one deigned to answer, Ashley continued, speaking loud enough for everyone in Elkton Falls to hear. "Only Father would book us into a lighthouse motel in the North Carolina mountains!"

As the owner and innkeeper of the "lighthouse motel,"

Alex had to fight to hide his smile. He knew how unusual most people found it to see a lighthouse in the foothills of the Blue Ridge Mountains, but to him, the original structure on the North Carolina Outer Banks was the one that looked oddly out of place without the lush green hardwood forest and the mountain's foothills surrounding it.

Cynthia Shays-Trask, the matriarch of the clan, was a slim older woman stylishly dressed in a designer outfit and sporting a graying closely cropped haircut. She said curtly, "Ashley, we are here because your father demanded it. That obese nightmare of a man has found a way to continue to spoil my life even beyond the grave."

Steven Trask, a young man in his midtwenties with neatly trimmed hair and a runner's physique said, "Mother, I won't have you speak of him that way, do you understand? It's time to put the past behind us." Unlike his sister and her outfit, Steven looked at home in a nicely tailored suit.

"Oh please, Steven," Ashley said. "It didn't do you the slightest bit of good being his favorite while he was alive, and it matters even less now. He can't hear you." All three shared the same hooked nose and prominent chin; the family resemblance was undeniable. Alex would have known they were related even without having the reservation book open in front of him. Though they were booked at the inn for the entire week, the group had refused to check in until Jase Winston, Alex's uncle and an attorney in town, arrived on the scene.

Jase had just recently moved back to Elkton Falls after retiring from a big law firm in Charlotte, and Alex had been glad for the chance to get reacquainted with his father's brother. Since Alex and his brother Tony had lost their parents, Jase had done his best to serve in their stead. Alex was glad his uncle had grown bored with retirement and had hung out his shingle in town. The man was coming alive again with cases to keep him occupied. He'd confided to

Alex that the two of them were a lot alike; they both dealt with the public and tried their best to serve them. Alex wondered if that was what his uncle had in mind when he'd gotten himself involved with this family.

Ashley rubbed her hand hesitantly across the top of an ornately carved black urn sitting on the table between them. "This is just like Father, popping up like this. It smacks of his annual Christmas postcards to the family. The only way he comes back to us from South America is in a jar full of ashes. He had some kind of nerve, leaving us all behind and sending a card once a year just to gloat about his new life."

Steven's face turned red as he snapped, "He just wanted us to know he was okay!" It was obvious his sister knew just what buttons to push to get a reaction from him.

Cynthia said sadly, "Steven, you always were such an innocent."

Ashley said, "He's not all that innocent. I could tell you stories about your precious little boy that would curl your toes, Mother."

Alex could tell that Steven was trying his best to ignore his sister's jab. "Can't we all just get along until Jase Winston gets here and reads the will?"

Ashley said, "Don't hold your breath hoping for family harmony, Steven. I for one refuse to honor a man who deserted me." Ashley frowned, then added, "I still don't understand why Donald and the children couldn't come with us this week. They're my family; they have every right to be here, too."

Cynthia said, "We've been over this a hundred times. The instructions stated clearly that no spouses or children were to attend. Your father wanted this to be just the three of us."

Alex had dusted the same spot on the front desk for the seventh time when Elise Danton came up behind him.

"Alex, I need you outside."

Elise served as the head of housekeeping at Hatteras

West. It was a glorified title, since there were just the two
of them on staff, but Alex knew he couldn't run Hatteras
West without her. He'd discovered that quickly enough
when Elise's father had suffered a major heart attack, and
Elise had been called back to his side. He hoped her parents
enjoyed good health for a long, long time. Alex was not at
all certain he could go through running the inn by himself
again.

"Is it important?" he asked. Alex would never have admitted to her that he'd been eavesdropping, but he couldn't
help himself. It was one of the fascinations of running the
inn, meeting such a vast variety of people.

"I don't think it can wait," Elise said as she motioned
him to the rear of the building.

When they got to the back hallway, Alex said, "Elise,
you aren't going to believe our newest guests. I was under
the impression that this was just going to be a normal family reunion when Jase booked their rooms, but they're here
for the reading of their father's will. And from the sound of
it, nobody but the man's son is all that upset he's gone."

Elise said, "Alex, I honestly don't care if they're here to
hold a seance to bring him back; they're paying guests, and
we need all of those we can get right now."

Alex knew too well how true that was. They'd nearly finished rebuilding the Main Keeper's Quarters a few months
before when they'd run out of the money raised from the
sale of emeralds found on the property. Unfortunately,
Emma Sturbridge, their staff gem hunter, still hadn't been
able to locate the source of the main vein of stones, if in
fact one even existed. The original discoverer had taken
that secret with her to the grave. Because of that, Hatteras
West, so named because of the exact replica of the Cape
Hatteras Lighthouse built beside the two keepers' quarters
that served as the inn, was heading dangerously close to
being in the red again.

Alex asked, "What's so important?"

"It's Vernum. I can't get the man to hold still long enough for me to have one word of conversation with him. You're the only one he'll talk to."

"Is there a problem with him?" Alex asked. Vernum, an older, rail-thin man with a heavy, flowing shock of white hair and a beard that bushed all around his face, had shown up at Hatteras West the week before, offering to do yard work and landscaping in exchange for one meal a day and a place to sleep. Alex had seen Vernum around Elkton Falls for the past few months, one day sweeping the parking lot at Buck's Grill and the next unloading trucks at Shantara's General Store. Sheriff Armstrong had talked to Vernum extensively upon showing up in Elkton Falls and had pronounced him harmless.

Alex had turned down the offer of landscaping, though he gave the stranger a good meal before he left. Instead of leaving, though, Vernum grabbed a pruning saw from the storage shed near the lighthouse and transformed some gnarled old oak trees Alex had been meaning to convert into firewood into beautifully sculpted showpieces.

Alex was convinced, and Vernum moved into the shed after refusing to sleep in any of the inn's empty rooms.

"There's no problem with Vernum," Elise explained. "I just hate the thought of him sleeping on a cot out in the shed."

"It's his choice, Elise. He seems happy out there. I can't *make* him come inside."

"Would you at least talk to him about it again? He listens to you."

"I will if I can find him," Alex said. He knew there was no point arguing with her. Once Elise made up her mind about something, it was nearly impossible to get her to change it. He had to admit she'd come up with many improvements since she'd arrived at the inn, none more popular than the continental breakfasts they now served every morning.

As Alex walked the grounds, he marveled at the work
Vernum had done in the short time he'd been at Hatteras
West. The unofficial arborist had thinned and pruned the
stand of oak and hickory trees that had grown up around
the lighthouse's base, transforming the area into a parklike
setting, revealing rather than obscuring the stone and brick
foundation. Even the copse of trees between the lighthouse
and Bear Rocks had never looked so good.

Alex finally found Vernum thinning the plantings around
the inn's main building.

"Got a second?" Alex asked.

Vernum looked startled as he realized Alex was standing
so close by. The man never failed to remind Alex of a
spooked horse, afraid to stay in one place too long, especially if anyone else was around.

"What can I do for you?" the man grumbled as he started
to move away.

"Elise is worried about you sleeping out in the shed. Are
you sure you don't want to move into the inn while you're
working here? We've got plenty of room right now."

Vernum called out over his shoulder, "I'm fine where I
am, thanks," as he disappeared into the copse of trees that
led to Bear Rocks.

Alex didn't have time to chase him down. He had an inn
to run. Peering inside through the glass, he could see the
Trask family still gathered around the patriarch's urn. It
was time to finish dusting that desk.

Hopefully, he hadn't missed much.

"Where is that man? Honestly, he shouldn't be wasting
our time like this," Cynthia said as she looked at her watch
for the hundredth time in the last fifteen minutes.

Steven asked, "Is there somewhere you need to be,
Mother? I thought we were *all* going to be staying the entire week."

"We are. That was your father's last request, and goodness knows, he'll probably come back and haunt anyone who tries to leave early. It's hard to imagine this dreadful town was his boyhood home. He never showed any interest in coming back while he was alive, so why in the world did he feel the need to drag us all here against our wills? I just wish we could get this part of the ordeal over with."

Ashley said, "Do you think it's possible he actually left us something valuable? The attorney hinted as much when I spoke with him on the telephone last week. Maybe he still has his stamp collection. That was worth a fortune twenty years ago."

Steven said, "I'm not so sure any of us deserve his money or anything else. He was gone a long time. Father carved out a new life for himself."

Cynthia said, "Donate your share to the poor if it eases your conscience, Steven. I for one earned every dime coming to me."

"We all did," Ashley said.

Steven stood abruptly. "It's getting a little stale in here. I need some fresh air."

Ashley snapped, "You'll just have to get it later, little Brother. Nobody's going anywhere until this lawyer shows up."

Alex watched openly as Steven and Ashley locked glares. The older sister ultimately won as Steven reluctantly slipped back into his seat.

Alex was so caught up in the exchange between the brother and sister that he was startled when Sheriff Armstrong walked into the inn. Normally, Alex knew it whenever a car approached on the gravel entrance outside. As the sheriff headed straight for Alex, the innkeeper had a sinking feeling in the pit of his stomach that he was there to deliver bad news. Armstrong didn't come to Hatteras West on many social calls; something had to have happened to dynamite him off his barstool at Buck's Grill.

"Afternoon, Sheriff," Alex said, trying to act more casual than he felt.

"Alex, I'm afraid I've got some bad news."

"What is it?" Alex asked as a wave of dread swept over him.

"It's your uncle. I'm afraid he's dead."

2

"Dead," **Alex said** softly. "Was it his heart?" His uncle Jase was getting on in years, but a part of Alex had believed the older man would live forever; he was so robust and full of life.

The sheriff shook his head and lowered his voice. "I wish I could tell you it was from natural causes, Alex, but it was nothing that tidy. Somebody killed Jase in his office."

"What?" Alex shouted. He knew he was causing a scene as everyone in the lobby stared at him, but he didn't care. Who would want to kill his sweet old uncle?

Elise was beside him in a heartbeat, touching his shoulder lightly. "What's wrong?"

"Somebody killed Jase," Alex said blindly. The words felt like ashes in his mouth. He turned to the sheriff and asked, "What happened?"

Armstrong looked as if he'd just swallowed a bug. "You know that miniature lighthouse he kept on his desk?"

"The brass one? Of course I do, I gave it to him for Christmas last year."

Armstrong said, "Well, somebody cracked him on the back of the skull with it. Irene said there were no prints, it was wiped down pretty good, but the points of impact match perfectly."

"So my lighthouse killed him," Alex said in disbelief.

"It could have been anything, Alex. The killer struck at the last minute and happened to grab that paperweight you bought him."

"I still can't believe it," Alex said haltingly.

Armstrong coughed once, then said, "I hate to do this right now, Alex, but I have to ask you something. Is there a Trask family staying with you?"

"They're over there," he said softly. "Jase was on his way out to talk to them. Do you think one of them might have had something to do with his murder?"

The sheriff ignored his question and walked over to the group.

Armstrong approached Cynthia and said, "Ma'am, are you Cynthia Trask?"

"Cynthia Shays-Trask," she corrected him. "What can I do for you, Officer?"

"It's Sheriff, ma'am. I'm afraid I've got some bad news for you. Jase Winston isn't going to be able to make his appointment with you today."

"Why not?" Ashley demanded.

Armstrong explained to the family, "I'm sorry to have to be the one to tell you folks this, but Jase Winston is dead."

Cynthia said, "What do you mean, he's dead? Who could possibly have a reason to kill an old country lawyer?"

"Now, I never said anything about murder," Armstrong said calmly.

Cynthia was unruffled by the intensity of his stare. "So he died from heart failure. He's still dead, isn't he?"

Alex fought the urge to strangle her.

Armstrong said, "No, as a matter of fact it *was* murder,

but I'm curious to know why you jumped to that particular conclusion."

"Sheriff, I live in a large city. When I hear someone has died, my mind jumps naturally to murder."

Steven asked, "Have you caught the killer?"

"Not yet," Armstrong admitted.

Ashley said, "I'm assuming you're not out here on a courtesy call. Sheriff, what exactly does this have to do with us?"

"That's what I was hoping you'd be able to tell me. The safe in his office was standing wide open, but as far as his secretary can tell, there's only one thing missing. She found an empty folder inside with the heading, 'The Last Will and Testament of Mathias Trask.' "

At that moment, Cynthia Shays-Trask fainted dead away.

Ashley cradled her mother's head in her lap. The matriarch quickly came around from her faint.

"Mother, are you all right?" Steven asked softly.

"I'm fine, Steven, it was just the shock of hearing the horrid news."

She hadn't fainted when she'd found out Jase was dead, Alex thought bitterly; it was the fact that the will was missing that had made her swoon.

Elise said, "Maybe you should drink this," as she offered Cynthia a glass of water.

After taking a healthy swallow, Cynthia said, "That's much better. Thank you, my dear." She turned to Armstrong and asked, "Now, why in the world would anyone want a copy of Mathias's will?"

"It's more serious than you think. Seems it was the only copy there was." Armstrong looked at the people gathered in the lobby and asked, "Would you all mind telling me where you were between six and nine this morning?"

Ashley exploded, "Do you mean to tell me we're suspects?

You're out of your mind, Sheriff. Do you honestly believe any of us would kill a stranger for our father's will?"

"The way I figure it, one of you didn't like the contents of that new will. I'm sure the thief didn't mean to kill old Jase, but it happened. If Mathias wrote one of you out of the will, I'm betting you figured a little cut of the pie was better than nothing at all. That's probably what's going to happen if this will doesn't turn up; most likely his worldly goods will get split up between the three of you. Now, one at a time, I need to know where you were."

Steven said, "Back up a second, Sheriff. We didn't know there was a will involving us until last week, or even that there was anything my father had that was worth leaving to any of us. How in the world could we have learned the contents of it in that short a time?"

Armstrong said, "Now, how can you prove something you didn't know? I've got just your word for it that your dad didn't have contact with any of you all along."

"All we got were postcards once a year, and they were always addressed to Mother," Steven said.

Armstrong shrugged. "I still need to know where you all were this morning."

Cynthia regained enough of her composure to say, "I'm afraid we won't be answering any of your questions until we consult with our attorney, Sheriff."

Armstrong said, "Unless you've got a Ouija board, I don't think you're going to have much luck doing that."

"We'll find new representation in Charlotte," Cynthia said stiffly.

Steven said, "I'm going to call Sandra Beckett. She'll know what to do."

Ashley said, "Honestly, Steven, do you think your old girlfriend is up to it?"

"She was never my girlfriend, Ashley; we just went to college together. Sandra's the only top-notch attorney I know anywhere near Elkton Falls, and I doubt we're going to get a decent lawyer from Charlotte willing to come up here. If Sandra isn't acceptable, do you have a better idea?" It was more of a challenge than a question.

"Just make the call," Cynthia said. "Let me meet her first, and then we'll decide."

As Steven went off to make the call, Alex still couldn't believe it. Jase was gone. And it wasn't the quiet, peaceful death he'd deserved, either. Alex realized long ago that Jase wouldn't be around forever, but losing him to murder was too much. Alex stood there in the lobby in a daze, Elise close by, not talking but giving him space and time to get used to the fact that his uncle was gone.

After Steven finished his call, the threesome sat with Sheriff Armstrong until Sandra came in fifteen minutes later, along with a young woman in her early twenties Alex didn't recognize.

Sandra ignored the family and walked straight to Alex. She wrapped her arms around him and said, "Alex, I'm so sorry. I know how much you loved your uncle."

"Thanks," he said as he returned her embrace. Elise had stayed close, but what he'd truly needed was a hug. He just hadn't realized it until Sandra had put her arms around him. They had dated for quite some time, but it turned out that Sandra was a much better friend than girlfriend.

When he and Sandra broke free, Alex noticed that Elise hadn't moved an inch away from him.

Sandra turned to the group and said, "Hello, Steven. It's good to see you again."

"Thanks for coming," Steven said.

"I'm afraid there's a problem. I won't be able to represent you in this matter. I've got a conflict of interest."

"What are you talking about, Sandra?" Steven asked.

Sandra motioned to the young woman with her and said, "I was supposed to meet with Jase this morning before he

came out here to read the will." She gestured toward the
woman, then said, "There's no easy way to say this. Everyone, I'd like you all to meet Julie Hart. She's Mathias's
other daughter."

"That's absurd," Cynthia said as she scowled at the
young woman. "Mathias Trask had only one daughter."

Julie looked as if she might cry, but she kept her bottom
lip steady as she said, "I only just found out myself. I'm
still having a hard time believing it."

Ashley said, "It's obvious she's a fake. Why, she doesn't
look like any of us."

Julie said simply, "I favor my mother."

Steven asked, "Is it true, then? Are you really our sister?"

Sandra stepped in. "It appears so. A few weeks ago, Julie
received a letter from Mathias's business manager in South
America. There was an explanation in the packet, then a
message from Mathias himself. There was no doubt in
Mathias Trask's mind she was his true daughter, and he
promised to treat her as such, in writing."

Cynthia scoffed. "A letter from a dead man will not stand
up in court. We'll have DNA tests run! She'll get nothing.
I'll make sure of that."

Sandra grinned. "Oh, I think she has a very good chance
of inheriting her share, Cynthia. With Mathias's declara-
tion, a DNA test isn't necessary. He wanted her to have a
full share in his will, regardless of her parentage, and she's
going to get everything she deserves. That's why I'm here,
to make certain that happens."

Steven said, "I can't believe you'd take her case against
me, Sandra. I thought we were friends."

Sandra said softly, "I'm sorry, Steven, but I'm friends
with most of Elkton Falls. I can't turn my back on a client
in need."

Ashley said defiantly, "There's more at issue here than a

case of hurt feelings. We won't stand for this. Do you understand?"

Julie started to say something, but Sandra put a hand on her arm and said, "It wasn't exactly the warm embrace my client was hoping for. We'll see you in court."

Sandra started to leave, but Julie lingered. Though her voice quivered, there was steel in her words. "I didn't do this on purpose. I'm just respecting my father's last wish."

"Whoever he may be," Cynthia said with cold dismissal in her voice.

Alex had watched the exchange as if he were seeing it through someone else's eyes. His own part of the tragedy was just starting to sink in. Nothing would be the same with Jase gone.

After Sandra and Julie left the inn, Elise asked, "Alex, is there anything I can do?" Her words brought him back as she lightly touched his shoulder.

He said, "I need to sit down."

She led him to a nearby chair in the lobby, and Alex slumped into it. Elise asked, "Would you like anything?"

"Water," Alex croaked.

He looked up at the sound of voices and suddenly realized that the Trasks were still there. He was going to have to pull himself together. Jase would have expected nothing less of him.

Alex heard Ashley ask, "So what happens now? I'm not about to let that imposter get her greedy little hands on Father's money."

Steven said, "You heard Sandra. If she's really our sister and Dad wanted her to inherit, how can we stand in her way?"

"Just watch me," Ashley said.

Cynthia looked at both her children. "Is it agreed, then? We fight this imposter's claim?"

Ashley nodded, but Steven refused to meet her gaze as he said, "I still don't think it's right. How can we go against his wishes?"

Cynthia said, "I'm warning you, Steven, if you don't stand with us against this woman, you'll be cut off yourself. I'll see to it."

Steven stood, and as he headed for the door he said, "Do what you have to, Mother."

After he was gone, Cynthia said to Ashley, "Don't worry, he'll come around. I'm sure Steven is wrong; we should have no problem getting representation from Charlotte here once they find out what's at stake. Now, let me call a few friends and see if I can come up with any recommendations. Dear, I'm afraid this isn't going to be as simple as we thought."

Ashley groaned. "So we're really going to have to stay here the full week?"

"At least that," Cynthia said with an air of resignation in her voice.

Elise gave Alex his water, then said, "Why don't I send the Trasks to a hotel in Hickory? You don't need to have guests around right now, especially ones tied in with all of this."

Alex said softly, "I want them to stay."

"It's too much," Elise insisted. "You need some time to deal with losing your uncle."

Alex said resolutely, "Check them in, Elise. I need to find out if one of them killed Jase. I can't do that if they're staying somewhere else."

Elise nodded. "Whatever you say."

As she checked the three guests into their rooms and showed them the way upstairs, Alex was happy to have the lobby back to himself. What had started out as an interesting situation had suddenly turned very ugly.

But one thing was certain. No one was leaving Hatteras West until Alex uncovered the truth about his uncle's murder.

3

"Tony, it's Alex."

He'd dreaded making the telephone call to his brother, but he really had no choice. As Alex dialed the number, he suddenly realized that they were the last of the Winstons, their particular branch of the family tree, anyway. Tony was a confirmed bachelor after a pair of failed marriages with no children from either union, now wedded only to his work, while Alex wondered if he'd ever get married himself. His relationship with Sandra, the last woman he'd dated seriously, was over and finished. The only woman he was interested in now was Elise, but she was engaged to a man in West Virginia, hundreds of miles away.

Tony said, "You don't have to identify yourself to me, Alex, I'd know that voice anywhere. So tell me, are you finally going to sell that white elephant you got saddled with?" Tony had opted for money instead of a half share of Hatteras West after their parents died, and he'd been urging Alex to get rid of the lighthouse in the mountains ever since.

"You know I'm not about to sell Hatteras West. It's home."

Tony said, "So why are you calling me in the middle of the day? I know it's not just to catch up on old times." That was Tony, always straight to the point. The two brothers had never gotten along all that well as children, much to their parents' chagrin. Growing older hadn't improved things between them, either. They were two strangers bound only by the common blood that ran through them.

"It's about Uncle Jase. He's dead."

There was a long pause on the other end of the line. Then Tony said softly, "So his heart finally gave out on him."

Alex took a deep breath, then said, "I wish it were that simple. Somebody killed him, Tony."

"Jase? Why?"

"The sheriff thinks it had something to do with a will Jase was supposed to execute today. There was only one copy, and now it's missing."

Tony asked, "Did he catch the killer?"

"Sheriff Armstrong is working on it."

"That's hardly reassuring. He's not exactly the South's greatest lawman, is he?"

Alex said, "Tony, he's a much better sheriff than you remember. Armstrong can handle this."

"Don't tell me you're not going to snoop around yourself. I know you too well. Get a room ready for me, Alex, I'm coming back to Elkton Falls."

Alex knew his brother would want to come back home, but it wasn't something he'd been looking forward to.

"I'll wait to handle the arrangements until you get here," Alex said.

"I'm on my way."

It would be odd for Alex to see his brother again, but he knew he'd manage to get through it somehow, for Jase's sake if nothing else. His mother and father had never understood the break between their sons, or the reasons for it.

Instead, they'd remembered the old days through the fog of wishful thinking, believing all had been happy and harmonious in the Winston household.

Alex knew better.

Elise walked up to him at the reservation desk and said, "Alex, is there anything I can do?"

"We'd better get room ten ready. My brother's going to stay with us."

She said, "It will be good for you to have your family here."

Alex shook his head. "I'm not so sure, Elise. We talk on the phone once or twice a year, but he hasn't set foot on the grounds of Hatteras West in six years."

"What happened between you?"

"Nothing; that's the whole point. We've always been strangers. Once our folks were gone, there was no need for us to even pretend to keep in touch. Elise, he may be my brother biologically, but Mor Pendleton is more of a brother to me than Tony ever has been."

Mor wouldn't be happy to see Tony back in Elkton Falls either. The two had been rivals in high school.

"I'll go freshen the room," Elise said.

Alex wanted to reach out to her, to hold her in his arms, to share some of his grief with her. But he couldn't burden her with his feelings for her, even now. At least not as long as she was still engaged to Peter Asheford. The man had looks, money, and Elise's heart.

But Alex was jealous only of the last part.

There was one place in the world Alex could go to lift his spirits: the top of the lighthouse. He only hoped no one was up there now; he needed to be alone.

As Alex ascended the steps that led to the top, his hand kept trailing against the cool, whitewashed stone of the tower. Hatteras West was the one constant in his life, al-

ways there, always watching over him. It was a part of him
in more ways than he could ever express, and it gave him a
very real comfort being within its shelter. Alex had taken
his very first breath inside the lighthouse on a stormy Hal-
loween night thirty-some years before, and the tower had
been linked to him ever since.

Climbing the 268 steps kept him in shape, though the
older he got, the longer the ascent took him. Alex didn't
even stop at the windows on his way up this time, needing
to get to the top as quickly as he could.

It was deserted on the observation deck that ran all the
way around the top. Alex leaned against the rail and looked
down on the nearly completed Main Keeper's Quarters,
with roof shingles that were still glossy and new, then let
his gaze drift over to nearby Bear Rocks. A lot had happened in his life, and Alex could tie nearly all of it to this
spot in the foothills of the Blue Ridge Mountains. He could
see the rolling ridges in the distance from his vantage point,
smoky with an azure haze. Jase had loved the lighthouse
nearly as much as Alex did, though he hadn't climbed it
since he'd come back to Elkton Falls. The stairs were just
too much for him.

But how he had enjoyed sitting on one of the rockers on
the front porch of the Dual Keepers' Quarters, staring up at
it.

At least his uncle had had the chance to come back home
before dying.

Alex heard footsteps behind him, and he suddenly
wished he'd locked the lighthouse doors on his way in.

When Alex turned to the door leading out to the platform, he was surprised to find Julie Hart standing there.

She tried to back out. "I'm sorry, I didn't know anyone
was up here."

Alex said, "You're welcome to stay, Julie. The lighthouse is open to everyone. You don't have to be a guest at
the inn to enjoy it."

She looked down at her feet. "I don't want to intrude. You just lost your uncle. I imagine you probably want to be alone, Mr. Winston."

He shook his head. "Call me Alex. I thought solitude was what I wanted, but to be honest with you, I wouldn't mind a little company right now." Alex surprised himself as he said it, realizing it was true. There was something about this young woman, a steel band behind the calm exterior, that appealed to him.

"Are you sure?" she asked gently.

"I'm positive. You are welcome here," Alex said as he moved back to the rail and leaned against it, looking again toward the Blue Ridge Mountains, taking in the majesty of it all. It was a view he could never grow tired of.

Julie joined him and gasped as she glimpsed the vista for the first time. "This place is awesome. I can't believe I never heard of it before."

"You can thank my wonderful public relations efforts for that," Alex said. "We're North Carolina's best kept secret," he added with a smile.

"Sorry, I didn't mean—"

Alex cut her off. "I was just teasing. As long as we have enough guests to break even, I'm a happy man." Alex paused, then added, "This can't be an easy time for you, either, having the Trasks turn on you like that."

Julie stared at the mountains a few moments before speaking. "You know, it was always just my mom when I was growing up, and when I lost her last year, I felt cut off from the rest of the world, like I wasn't really connected to anybody else. It sounds crazy, doesn't it?"

Alex shook his head as he said, "When I lost my folks, I felt like I'd been cut adrift. I've got a brother I don't really know, so Jase was all that was left of what I considered my real family. For the first time in my life, I feel like there's just me."

Julie moved closer, though still not touching him, and

Alex felt warmed by her presence. "So you do know how I feel. When your uncle's letter came, the first thing I thought of was that I wasn't alone anymore. I wanted to introduce myself to the Trasks right away, but Sandra said I should wait." A tear crept down her cheek as she added, "It wasn't the family reunion I'd been hoping for. Alex, I don't care about the money or anything else my father might have left me. I wanted *him*, something I never had growing up. But the Trasks just think I'm trying to steal something that I'm not entitled to." Alex watched as she battled her emotions.

It was an easy motion to put his arm around Julie, and she buried her head in his chest and cried.

Alex said softly, "Don't give up on them. I think Steven might come around. You just may have to give them all some time. I'm sure it was quite a shock for them."

Julie pulled back, wiping the tears from her face. As she leaned up to kiss him on the cheek, Alex heard a footfall on the stairwell and looked up in time to find Elise there.

"Sorry, I didn't mean to interrupt," she said.

Julie blushed, adding to whatever Elise imagined she saw. Then Alex suddenly realized he had nothing to explain, nothing to feel guilty about. After all, Elise was the one who was engaged to somebody else. Though they'd shared many meals together, they'd never even been on a real date.

So why did he feel so guilty?

Julie said, "I was just leaving. Thanks for the talk, Alex, it did me a world of good."

"You're more than welcome."

Elise didn't follow Julie down but instead lingered at the top of the observation platform, as if waiting for him.

He was surprised to find himself explaining, "She was crying, so I offered her what comfort I could."

Elise shook her head. "That's not why I came looking for you. Alex, there's something I need to tell you. I'm sorry about the timing, but I can't do anything about it."

"You're leaving, aren't you," he said woodenly. The thought had been constantly in the back of his mind since Elise had first come to Hatteras West. She was more qualified than he was to run the inn, with her degree in hotel management from a major university. It was just a matter of time before she got bored with the drudge work at Hatteras West.

She looked genuinely surprised by the notion. "No, I'll stay here as long as you want me. I thought you knew that. I love this place."

Alex couldn't hide the relief that swept through him. "So what's on your mind?"

Elise bit her lip, then said, "It's Peter Asheford. He's coming to Elkton Falls."

Alex felt a wrenching in his gut. He'd always hoped that as long as Elise and Peter stayed apart, there might be a chance for him someday. It looked like that chance was gone.

"How can he do that? I thought he ran some great company he owned and couldn't afford to leave it."

Elise said, "It was just a toy for him, and he got bored with it, so he sold the business. Peter's family has serious money, Alex."

An unpleasant thought struck him. "Is he staying with us at the inn when he comes?"

She shook her head. "You don't understand. Alex, he's not visiting. Peter is moving to Elkton Falls to be closer to me." She held his gaze a moment, then added, "I just thought it was something you should know."

Before Alex could say another word, Elise left him alone on the observation deck with nothing but his thoughts. Just when he thought life couldn't get any more complicated, it had managed to throw him another curve, and this one was a real dinger.

Elise had originally moved to Elkton Falls to get away from her job and her fiancé, to find time to decide what she really wanted out of life. A part of him had been hoping the new plan would include him.

But with Peter Asheford on the scene again, Alex realized that was probably never going to happen. Most likely Peter would persuade her to leave, and that would be the end of that.

It was time to move on with his life. Alex knew he couldn't wait around for Elise forever. He'd have to accept the fact that they'd most likely be nothing more than friends. Besides, romance should be the last thing on his mind at the moment. He had a murderer to catch, and Alex had a sneaking suspicion that the killer was lurking somewhere near Hatteras West.

4

"The place looks great," Tony said as he walked into the lobby of the Dual Keepers' Quarters the next day, the only part of the inn fit for guests at the moment. "I can't believe you're rebuilding the main quarters. It must be costing you a fortune."

Alex looked at his brother and smiled. "There are more things in life than money, Tony. It's really important to me to restore the place to all its glory."

"And you actually got someone to loan you the money for the reconstruction? I know your insurance couldn't have covered all you lost in the fire. Smiley O'Reilly is still using actuarial charts from the 1950s."

Alex couldn't deny that. The money from his insurance policy had barely covered some of the new furniture he'd needed, but Alex wasn't about to admit to his brother that there was the possibility of an emerald-rich vein somewhere on the property. He knew what Tony's reaction would be without even asking; dump the inn and sell the land for all he could get. He'd never felt the pull Alex did for Hatteras West.

Tony looked out the nearest window and said, "Some homeless guy's out there, Alex. You really should run him off before he drives your guests away."

Alex laughed. "That's my arborist. His name is Vernum, and he's a whiz at landscaping, too."

"You never could resist taking in strays, could you? You're just as soft as Mom was."

"Thanks, that's nice of you to say," Alex replied, intentionally misinterpreting the jab in the comment.

Elise walked in with an armful of fresh towels. She put them on one corner of the check-in desk as Tony moved toward her. "You must be Elise Danton. I've heard so many wonderful things about you, it's so nice to finally meet you." For a second, Alex thought Tony was going to kiss her hand, but he somehow managed to restrain himself.

Elise smiled lightly. "It's nice meeting you, Tony."

Tony said smoothly, "Alex was just going to show me to my room, but if you've got a second, I'd much rather have you take me."

Elise retrieved the towels, then said levelly, "I think you should go with Alex. I know you two have a lot to discuss."

Alex tried to hide his smile. Sometimes he forgot how stunning Elise was, with her long chestnut hair and gentle green eyes. She was an old hand at rebuffing advances, and she'd sized Tony up in a heartbeat.

As she walked away, Tony said, "I'm starting to see why the inn life is so appealing to you, Alex."

Alex brushed his brother's comment off with a wave of his hand. "You're out of your league, Tony. Her fiancé's just moved to Elkton Falls, and he's got more money and charm than either one of us will ever manage in a lifetime."

Tony smiled broadly. "Ah, but she's not married yet, now is she? You know how I love a challenge. I'm not giving up that easily."

"You never did," Alex said, shaking his head. Some things never changed, and his brother was at the top of the list. There was no denying Tony could be charming when it suited him, but he doubted his brother could make an impression on Elise. It might even be fun to watch, Alex thought as he showed his brother to his room. Though Tony knew the place as well as Alex did, the innkeeper's instinct in him demanded he escort his brother.

Alex asked, "Do you want to get settled first, or should we go into town and take care of the arrangements for Jase's funeral now?"

"I didn't think you could leave the inn," Tony said as he started unpacking his bag.

Alex said, "Elise can handle things while I'm gone. If it's all the same to you, I'd like to get this over with as quickly as we can."

Tony agreed. "It's probably the best thing to do. Uncle Jase never was fond of drawing things out. Let me grab a quick shower, and I'll be ready to go in twenty minutes."

"I'll meet you in my office downstairs. I've got some work I need to do before we go."

Tony smiled. "That's my little brother, ever diligent. See you soon."

Before Alex could get within a hundred feet of his office, Cynthia Shays-Trask cornered him in the lobby. "Mr. Winston, I need to speak with you. It's rather urgent."

"What can I do for you, Ms. Trask?"

"I don't know how to put this delicately, but this is the time for boldness. I saw you with your arms around that imposter at the top of your odd little lighthouse earlier today, and I want you to know that I won't stand for any foolishness from you butting into my family's business. Do you understand me?"

If there was one thing Alex was generally good at, it was dealing with people. He had learned long ago that there were as many types of guests at Hatteras West as there were people in the outside world. Some thrived on rudeness, even seemed to demand it in return, while others had to be soothed and coddled over the course of their entire stay, calling for attention relentlessly. Others came up with the oddest requests, expecting—no, demanding—that they be met or the world would end. One of the first skills Alex had acquired as an innkeeper was how to handle just about everyone who passed through his doors.

With Cynthia Shays-Trask, he didn't really care which group she belonged to; all he knew was that she could have had something to do with his uncle's death.

"What I do here at Hatteras West is my business," he said briskly, trying to skate past her.

"When it concerns my family, it becomes my business," she said forcefully.

Alex said, "You heard Sandra; Julie is a part of your family now. Your son and daughter have a half sister, whether any of you have the decency to acknowledge it or not."

Cynthia's eyes flared. "So you don't deny it? You are in league with that tart?"

Alex said flatly, "The only thing I care about is who killed my uncle. Not that it's any of your business, but Julie needed someone to talk to today, and I happily obliged. I don't have the slightest interest in getting involved in your family's problems. Now, if you'll excuse me, I've got work to do."

Alex tried to get around her, but Cynthia put a hand lightly on his arm. There was a look of repentance on her face, though Alex couldn't help wondering if it was rehearsed. There was even something that rang false about the woman's indignation.

"Alex, forgive my outburst. I forgot how you must be grieving. It's just that when my children's welfare is at stake, I can be a bit of a mother bear. Again, please forgive me."

"There's nothing to forgive," Alex said, trying to keep his tone level. "Now, if you'll excuse me, I really must get to work. I've got a funeral to plan."

Was that a glimmer of real guilt peeking through Cynthia's carefully constructed facade? It happened too quickly to tell, gone as fast as it had appeared. She said, "I am truly sorry for your loss."

"Thanks," Alex muttered as he finally escaped and headed for the refuge of his tiny office.

Alex found Mor Pendleton sitting behind his desk, his feet propped up on top of a stack of paperwork and leaning back in his chair.

Mor stood up abruptly when Alex came in. "Sorry to hear about Jase. Anything I can do?"

Alex said, "Thanks, but Tony's helping me with everything. He's up in room ten now, unpacking."

"And how is he? I was surprised when I saw him in town last week. At least I thought it was him." There was still a hint of steel in Mor's voice whenever he talked about Tony.

"He's the same as always, but you've got to be wrong about Tony being in Elkton Falls. It would take an act of Congress to get him back here. I'm just sorry it took Jase's murder. Enough of that. How's bachelor life treating you now that Emma has deserted you?" Mor had been dating Alex's resident gem hunter, Emma Sturbridge, since she'd moved to town. They'd come close to breaking it off earlier but had somehow managed to patch things back together well enough to continue their relationship.

"Emma called yesterday. She got to Georgia just fine. Why she has to go prospecting for gold all the way over there when we've got gold in North Carolina is beyond me. That lady's actions defy all logic. I just don't understand women."

Alex smiled slightly. "Well, if you ever do, be sure to share your wisdom with me."

Mor laughed. "You'll be the second to know." His expression turned somber as he asked, "You want me to call her back home, what with all that's going on here?"

As comforting as it would be to have Emma Sturbridge nearby, Alex decided it wouldn't be fair to bring her back from her first vacation since she'd moved to Elkton Falls. "No, I'll be okay."

Mor glanced at his watch. "Just thought I'd ask. Well, I'd better take off. Les wants to talk about something over lunch. It's got to be serious; he even offered to pay." Lester Williamson was the other half of Mor or Les, the handyman duo that kept Elkton Falls up and running.

Alex asked, "You sure you aren't just ducking out before Tony gets downstairs?"

Mor grinned. "That, too." The smile disappeared as he added, "Listen, if there's anything I can do, you just let me know." He hugged Alex fiercely, then released him just as quickly. It was the way of the true Southern men he knew, mostly uncomfortable with embraces, but offering them when they were needed. Mor was one of the small circle of Alex's true friends, someone he could call at three A.M. and know that the man would come running without a single question why.

Just like a real brother should do.

Alex was still staring at the papers spread out on his desk, not really seeing them, as he was lost in his thoughts of Jase, when Tony walked in.

"This can wait if you've got work to do, Alex. Believe me, I know what it's like to be stuck behind a wall of paperwork."

Alex looked up and said, "No, we need to take care of this today. Sandra's expecting us at her office, and we've got to swing by the funeral home, too."

Outside, Alex headed for his old Ford pickup, but Tony pointed to his BMW. "Why don't we take my car? To be honest with you, I'm not sure I want to ride around in that truck of yours."

Alex reluctantly slid into the passenger seat of the silver sportster. It was close enough to Sandra's to be its twin, and he marveled that she'd ever ended up dating him instead of his older brother. Truth be told, the two of them had a lot more in common than she and Alex ever had.

Tony said, "Now this is what I call a smooth ride. It beats that old jalopy of yours, doesn't it?"

Alex said, "It's never let me down yet, and my truck's got real character." He'd promised himself to do his best to get along with Tony, no matter what.

Tony held up one hand. "Just kidding. I haven't seen old man Crassey in years. I guess he'll be handling the funeral arrangements. He's the only man I ever knew who owned six black suits."

"You haven't heard? Jack's running the mortuary now, Tony."

"So the old man finally retired and let his son take over. Did Crassey move to Florida like he'd always threatened to?"

Alex shook his head sadly. "Nothing as happy as all that. He died two years ago in a car wreck. I fired up the Fresnel lens for him the night of the funeral just long enough to keep from getting into trouble with the town council. A lot of the older town residents still think of it as a sign of respect."

"It's too bad the old guy didn't make it to live out his dream. I always liked him. Well, here we are."

They parked in front of Sandra's law office, a quaint old house with gingerbread trim and scalloped shingles painted in Victorian hues. The building was right on Main Street, down a block from Shantara's General Store and across the road from Irene's beauty parlor. To Dye For was painted a bright shade of neon blue, in stark contrast with Sandra's more traditional color choices.

Alex heard someone calling his name as he got out of the BMW.

It was Sheriff Armstrong, just across the street at the beautician's. "Alex, got a minute? I need a word with you."

Alex turned to his brother. "Tony, why don't you go ahead and get started with Sandra. I'll catch up with you in a minute."

After Tony disappeared inside Sandra's building, Alex walked over to Armstrong and asked, "Any leads on Jase yet, Sheriff?"

To Alex's surprise, he nodded. "Irene found something odd, and she wanted you to have a look. She's doing Mrs. Grishaber's perm right now. I know this isn't the best time in the world for you, but I could use a minute if you've got it to spare."

Alex knew he needed to be with Tony in Sandra's office, but what he wanted more than anything else was to help find Jase's killer.

Tony would just have to get along without him.

"I'm right behind you."

5

Irene Wilkins was Elkton Falls' crime scene investigator as well as the owner of To Dye For, the biggest beauty shop in town. Alex had been skeptical about her criminology abilities until she'd taken top honors in a regional competition, beating out several other, more experienced forensic professionals.

The beauty shop was filled with the smell of chemicals as Alex and the sheriff walked in. Irene said, "I'll be with you boys in a minute."

Armstrong coughed into his handkerchief as he said, "We'll just wait outside, if it's all the same to you."

Irene smiled. "You always were the sensitive type, Ducky."

As the two men walked back out into the fresh air, Alex said, "So what's this clue you want me to see?"

"I'm not sure if it's one or not; that's the whole point. But you know Irene, when she gets something in her head, there's no stopping her. Why don't we wait for her?"

Alex asked, "Do you have any real leads, Sheriff? Any suspects at all?"

"You know me, Alex, I suspect everybody at first. There's the entire Trask family to start with: Ashley, Steven, and momma Cynthia. Any one of them could have done it. Then there's this mysterious daughter nobody knew about until yesterday. To be honest with you, at the moment, I'm leaning toward her, myself."

Alex couldn't imagine sweet Julie bashing Jase's head in, not after she'd cried in his arms at the top of the lighthouse. But Alex was the first to admit that he wasn't the most objective person when it came to judging the women around him.

He asked, "Is there any reason in particular you think she might have done it?"

"That letter from Jase bothers me, Alex. Where's all this proof that she's really his daughter? I keep asking Sandra, but she won't show me one shred of evidence that's convincing. Says she doesn't want to show her hand before she has to, and I can't make her, not at this point, anyway."

"Do you have a theory why Julie would want to get her hands on the will?"

Armstrong hitched at his belt as he said, "What if there was something in there that contradicted what she's been claiming? If she knew about it, she'd have every reason in the world to want that particular document to disappear."

"But she just found out she was Trask's daughter a few weeks ago," Alex protested.

"So she says," Armstrong said as the beauty shop door opened.

Irene said, "Come on in, boys, I've got a few minutes before I have to get back to work."

The beautician led them past the salon part of the building back to her office. Irene had the oddest assortment of paperweights on her desk he'd ever seen, from a pipe tipped with red paint to a blue-steel revolver to a thin wire garrote.

Irene smiled broadly at Alex, though her eyes were reddened. The chemicals she worked with must play havoc with her senses. "Some collection, isn't it? Don't worry, none of these were used for actual murders." She added with a flourish, "at least not that I know about."

Alex asked, "What's this clue I'm supposed to look at?"

Irene went to her filing cabinet, opened the bottom drawer and pulled out the torn edge of an envelope safely ensconced in a clear plastic baggie. The jagged tear showed just the tip of an Old English letter.

It was either a *T* or a *J*, as far as Alex could tell.

"What's the significance of it, Irene?" Alex asked as he flipped over the baggie holding the scrap of paper to examine the pristine back side.

"Well, it's bound to mean something. I found it in the right cuff of Jase's pants. I'm thinking it might have happened during a struggle in his office."

Armstrong asked, "You ever seen anything like that before, Alex?" as he tapped the bag.

"Not that I can recall. Do you even know which letter it stands for?"

Irene blew her nose, then said, "The boys in Raleigh are running a check for me; I faxed them a photocopy. Alex, I searched that office floor on my hands and knees, but I couldn't find a single matching piece of the envelope it came from. My best guess is the killer may have taken it with him."

Alex asked the sheriff, "So you're thinking it's a *T* and it stands for Trask?"

He shook his head. "Nope, I'm leaning toward it being the tip of a *J*, and that would be Julie Hart. I've seen women use their first-initial monogram before, Alex, and she had motive enough."

"I just don't see her as a killer, Sheriff. You can't afford not to look at the Trask family, too."

Armstrong patted his shoulder. "Alex, you always did

have a weakness for the ladies. They murder too, you know."

"I just don't think she did it."

Armstrong said, "Now, don't go snooping around into this, Alex. I'm on the case. I know how much you like to investigate, but you're too close to this. Trust me, I'll find out who killed your uncle."

Alex started to say something, but Irene cut him off. "Why don't you two take this outside? I've got to get back to Mrs. Grishaber." She dabbed at her eyes again, and they took the hint.

Armstrong and Alex walked out front again. Tony was beckoning to him from the front steps of Sandra's building across the street, but before he left, Alex said, "At least talk to the Trasks, Sheriff. They'll be at the inn all week."

Armstrong shrugged. "I'll be out tomorrow first thing in the morning. I can talk to them then. Any chance of getting one of Elise's famous omelets?"

"You'll have to ask her yourself," Alex said as he hurried across the street. He couldn't believe the sheriff was narrowing his focus in on just Julie. That was his style: pick a suspect and go after them until he had enough evidence for an arrest, or until he decided to move on. Alex was certain the sheriff had agreed to interview the Trasks as much for the hoped-for omelet as for possible clues in the case.

Well, Alex was just going to have to keep giving him nudges in the right direction.

If only he knew which way that was.

Tony met Alex on the steps outside Sandra's office. As they walked into the waiting room together, Tony said, "She's on a long-distance telephone call, and her secretary just stepped out," as he gestured back to her office. "Did the sheriff have anything worthwhile to say?"

Alex considered telling Tony about the torn envelope,

but without more information, there wasn't any real way to determine if it was even a clue. Besides, he didn't want to put himself in the position of defending the sheriff to his brother again. "He's working hard on the case," Alex said.

"Let's hope he's working smart, too."

Sandra came out a minute later and said, "Sorry about that. Shall we begin?"

They followed Sandra into her office, and Alex glanced at her diplomas proudly displayed on the wall next to her desk. The entire room was decorated in Bob Timberlake furniture, with a beautifully crafted desk and matching chair as elegant as any found in New York City. There was a richness there, a confident aroma of success in the place, that matched Sandra perfectly.

Sandra picked up a document on top of her desk, studied it a moment, then said, "This is all fairly straightforward, gentlemen, but Jase wanted the reading of his will executed as soon after his death as possible. Let me say again how sad I am about this entire business."

Tony said tersely, "Yes, I can understand your displeasure when the people of Elkton Falls start killing attorneys."

"That's not what I meant at all, Tony. Jase was a good man, someone I was proud to call a friend of mine. In fact, we handled each other's wills."

"Tony, will you let Sandra do her job?" Alex remembered how he'd ended up dating Sandra instead of Tony back in high school. She'd rebuffed his older brother's last-minute invitation to the prom, going with Alex instead, since he had asked her first. There had been a wall between Sandra and Tony ever since.

Alex and Sandra stopped dating after she went off to college, not picking up again until a few years before Elise first came to Elkton Falls.

Sandra took another lengthy document from the folder

on her desk as she said, "The arrangements for Jase's funeral are easy, in that there isn't going to be one."

Before Tony could protest, Sandra went on. "Jase has gone into great detail about the farewell he wanted. His final request was that you both scatter his ashes from the top of the lighthouse one hour past sunset as the beacon rotates one minute for every year of his life." Sandra tapped another document as she added, "Somehow Jase got the town council to approve it. I still don't know how he managed it; he must have called in every marker he had."

Alex found it incredible that his uncle had managed the variance even then. Alex had been fined three times over the past two years for turning the beacon on over and above the once-a-year Lighthouse Lighting ceremony that had turned into a festive event for folks from seven counties.

Sandra went on. "The scattering of the ashes is to happen only after the executor, that's me, spends quite a considerable amount of cash on a farewell party, including balloons, party hats, and streamers, as well as an extravagant buffet and a dance band. Jase wanted to go out in style, and he's going to get exactly what he wanted. Is Monday night good for you two?"

"Monday night's fine," Alex said, and Tony reluctantly agreed. The Hatteras West Inn was going to host the oddest funeral Alex had ever heard of, but it was just like Jase to go out with his own sense of humor at the forefront.

As Tony gestured to the open document, he said, "What about the rest of it? Are you going to finish reading the will now?"

Alex said, "Come on, Tony, there's no rush. Why don't we wait until after the funeral? We can't really call it that, can we, and I refuse to call it a party. Maybe *send-off* is the best term for it."

Sandra said, "I'm sorry, Alex, but Jase wanted the entire will read as soon as possible, and seeing that you two are the main parties mentioned with specific bequests, we might as well go forward."

She picked up the document again and began to read aloud. "To my nephew Tony, who always valued money above nearly everything else, I leave three-quarters of the bonds and stocks in my estate."

"Just how much money are we talking about here?" Tony asked.

Alex said, "Tony, is that really an appropriate question right now?"

Alex's brother didn't look the least bit fazed by the comment. "So money matters to me. Jase knew it; I've never hidden it from anybody. After I've made my fortune, you'll still be stuck running a broken-down old inn." He tapped Sandra's desk with his fingers. "So, how much do I get?"

Sandra frowned as she looked through a stack of papers still in the folder. Finally she said, "As close as I can figure it, you'll be getting around one hundred thousand dollars."

Tony's smile was substantial. "Good old Uncle Jase. He understood me after all."

Alex had been surprised by the revelation that Tony would receive the lion's share of the inheritance. He'd always thought he and his uncle had shared a special bond. Alex was more hurt that it hadn't been an even split than upset over the fact that his inn could have really used the healthy influx of cash. Hatteras West would find a way to get by, no matter what. It had to; it was his life.

Sandra continued. "To my nephew Alex, I leave my most prized possessions, including my collection of books as well as the entirety of my remaining real property. I'm sorry it's not more, but remember this always, Alex; our bond always went beyond money."

Tony slapped Alex on the shoulder. "Sorry about that, Alex. Well, at least you get twenty-five grand out of the deal."

Sandra frowned gently, then said, "I'm sorry Alex, but

that's not the case. Jase willed the remainder of his money to the Elkton Falls Preservation Society. You know how much he loved this old town."

Tony stood and said, "Jase was something, wasn't he? Alex, are you ready to go back to the inn? We can deal with the other stuff later."

"Why don't you head back without me, Tony? I'll catch a ride and be out later."

Tony slapped him on the shoulder. "Come on, don't be a sore loser about this. I'm sorry you got screwed, but that's the way it goes sometimes."

Sandra piped up, "Tony, why don't you do as Alex suggests and go on. I'll give him a ride out to the inn myself."

Tony shrugged his shoulders. "Suit yourself. See you there, Alex."

And then he was gone. Alex wouldn't have been surprised to see him skipping as he left the office.

Sandra said, "Oh, Alex, I'm so sorry. I tried to talk Jase out of this division of property, but he was adamant about setting things up this way."

Alex sat there staring at his hands, and then a slow smile spread across his face.

Sandra said, "What in the world do you have to smile about?"

Alex chuckled softly. "It just hit me. You read the will yourself, Sandra. Jase gave Tony the money because that's all he ever cared about. You know how Jase felt about his books! They were his pride and joy. No, I'm satisfied with the will."

Sandra looked at him a long ten seconds, then said, "Alex, you're truly something, you know that?"

Alex laughed softly, "Thanks, Sandra, I appreciate that. You don't have to give me a ride out to Hatteras West, I know how busy you must be. I'll find a way to get back out there."

She shuffled a few papers on her desk, then said, "Nonsense, I'd love to take you home. In fact," she said as she stood, "I'm ready to go, if you are."

Alex said, "That's just it. I'd like to spend a little time at Jase's first, by myself. To be honest with you, it might help me say good-bye in my own way. I'm not sure I'm all that comfortable with the party he's planned, so I need to do it my way first."

Sandra sat back down in her chair. "I understand completely. Let's do this. I'll give you an hour over there, and then I'll come by to pick you up, and we'll eat at Mamma Ravolini's before we head back to the inn. My treat. What do you say?"

"I say it sounds great, but I have an inn full of people at the moment. I don't feel right about just leaving them alone."

Sandra said, "So let Elise take care of them. You deserve a break, Alex. Can you even remember the last time you took a day off, let alone a vacation?"

Alex found himself agreeing, as Sandra handed him a set of keys. "These are to the house. I'm afraid you'll have to have everything out in five days. The lease is up, and I couldn't get the landlord to extend it for you. He's got a hot prospect who's buying it from him."

"That'll be fine. I'm not going to move anything today. I just want to look around a little."

"See you in an hour then," Sandra said as Alex headed out.

He stopped at Sandra's secretary's desk and asked to borrow the telephone.

Elise answered on the second ring.

"Hatteras West Lighthouse and Inn," she said. He never tired of hearing her say it.

"Hi, it's me. Can you handle things there for a while? I've got some things in town I need to take care of."

"How did it go with Sandra?"

Alex took a deep breath, then said, "Tony got the money, but I got Jase's books."

Elise said, "Oh Alex, I'm so sorry."

"I'm not," he said. "Things couldn't have gone any better."

On the way over to Jase's cottage, Alex realized that his uncle had indeed given him the perfect gift. Long after Tony had spent every dime of his inheritance, and Alex knew that wouldn't take long, given his brother's propensity to burn up cash, Alex would have Jase's presence still with him, in the form of the books they both so loved.

It was worth more to him than ten times what Tony had gotten, and Alex wondered if Tony would ever realize just how much he'd lost today.

Probably not, and that was the saddest part of all.

6

The first thing Alex did when he got to Jase's rental house was to open the windows and let some fresh air in. Jase liked to keep things closed up, but Alex needed the warm breezes and sunshine. Located just two blocks from Sandra's office, the house was a quaint little cottage that had seen better days, tucked among businesses and houses alike in a mishmash that was much of Elkton Falls. The town had been nearly built by the time the elders got around to thinking about zoning. It made a happy mix, as far as Alex was concerned.

With just four small rooms, the cottage had most likely been perfect for the widower Jase. The elder Winston had rented it furnished with simple but serviceable furniture, and the only real way to tell that Jase had lived there at all was the explosion of books everywhere. Alex had only spent a handful of hours there since his uncle had moved back to Elkton Falls. Jase had loved the lighthouse so much, he was always eager to come out to Hatteras West.

Surveying the sheer volume of books around him, Alex

realized it was going to be an arduous task to pack up all of
Jase's books and personal items, but he'd worry about that
after the send-off. For the moment, he just wanted to be
near his uncle's things. Alex moved into the tiny bedroom
to find the room curiously nearly devoid of books. The
place was neat, the bed was made, and there was no mess in
sight. It was almost as if Jase had known he wouldn't be
coming back.

There was a thick accordion folder full of papers on the
room's simple desk, and Alex decided he should take those
back to Hatteras West with him when he left. There might
be something important that needed to be addressed. He
also found Jase's collectibles box, something he'd seen
around his uncle his entire life. Alex lifted the lid with
bated breath as he stroked the sides of the box, made from
the now-gone American chestnut tree. He was tempted to
sit down and go through his uncle's treasures. At the top,
Alex could see a Confederate bullet, a few Indian arrow-
heads, and the fragment of meteor Jase had. There were
chips of emerald there, of no real cash value, but ones Jase
had found himself in Hiddenite. There were, just like the
last time Alex had seen the box, a handful of the steel pen-
nies Jase loved. It was a box full of memories, more than
anything else. He could spend all evening going through it,
but there wasn't time at the moment. Alex tucked the box
under one arm and walked over to the nightstand. He
picked up the last book Jase would ever read. It was titled
The Treasure Below. Just then, he heard someone else in the
house!

Throwing the book on top of the bed, Alex moved
quickly toward the door. As he approached, he heard something fall in the living room.

"Who's there?" Alex shouted as he raced through the
doorway, the papers, the collection box and the book now
forgotten.

He got into the hallway just in time to see the front door

slam shut. Running to it, Alex tripped over a pile of books that had been upset by the intruder. By the time he got to his feet and jerked the door open, whoever had invited themselves in was gone. There were a dozen stores nearby that the intruder could have ducked into, and Alex knew he'd never find the interloper.

As Alex stepped back inside, he wondered why anyone would just walk into Jase's house uninvited. What could he, or she for that matter, have been looking for?

Alex started leafing through the books that had been disturbed. There was nothing out of the ordinary that he could see as he restacked them. Had it been an accident that they'd been spilled, or had the would-be thief been looking for something in particular?

He was still on his knees in the living room when there was a knock on the door.

It was Mor, standing just in the shadows, a weary frown on his face.

Mor said, "Listen, I hate to interrupt you, but do you have a second? I really need to talk to you. I know the timing stinks, but it's important."

Alex felt his heart race. "Is something wrong?"

"No, no. At least I don't think so. Not yet, anyway. Well, maybe, it depends on how you look at it."

"That certainly clears things up," Alex said with a smile.

His best friend didn't respond to the jab, and that's when Alex knew just how serious Mor was.

Alex walked out onto the abbreviated porch with Mor close behind, and the two men sat on the steps out front, avoiding each other's gaze.

Mor said, "Sandra told me I could find you over here, but she didn't want me to come. She said you needed some time alone. That woman's an overprotective hen when it comes to you. I don't remember her being so careful of your feelings when the two of you were dating."

"Sandra means well, but I don't have to have perfect solitude to say good-bye. What's up?"

Mor took a deep breath, then said heavily, "It's Les. He's talking about retiring again."

Alex knew Mor's partner talked about quitting their business a dozen times a year. Though the man was in his early seventies, he could probably run circles around folks half his age. "Mor, he's been threatening to quit forever. What makes this time any different?"

Mor rocked back as he said, "This is the first time he's ever been serious enough to offer to sell his share of the business to me. Seems he's found a new girlfriend, and he's thinking about leaving Elkton Falls with her and seeing the world."

That was news to Alex. Normally, in a place as small as Elkton Falls, it was as tough keeping a secret as it was to repeal the law of gravity. The kudzu vine was faster than any regular grapevine known to man.

"So who is this mystery woman?" Alex asked.

"I have no idea," Mor admitted, "but I think she lives in Saint Dunbar." Saint Dunbar was a town twenty miles away, closer to the mountains than Elkton Falls. It was in such an odd place geographically that it could be raining in Elkton Falls and snowing up a storm in Saint Dunbar. That could explain the mystery. Saint Dunbar was far enough away to be out of the reach of Elkton Falls radar. The kudzu vine only traveled so far when it came to gossip.

"So, what are you going to do?"

Mor scratched his chin. "I can come up with most of the money, but Les would have to take a note for the rest. Not that he'd mind, but I hate carrying paper like that. But that's not the real problem, Alex. To be honest with you, the whole thing is just too permanent for my taste."

"What's Emma think about all of this?" Since Mor and

Emma had started dating, she'd become a very real part of the handyman's life, Alex knew.

"She doesn't know about it, and I'm not sure I want to tell her. Not just yet, anyway." Mor stared at his hands a moment, then said, "She's already been badgering me about my lack of commitment to anything, and now this comes up."

Alex patted Mor's shoulder. "So where does that leave you?"

"Alex, I swear I don't know. When I lost that scholarship and came back home, I kind of fell into working with Les by accident more than design. Even though he made me partner a few years later, I still felt like I could pick up any time I wanted to and leave, do you know what I mean? Is Elkton Falls all I'm ever going to know? There's a whole world out there, my friend, and I'm afraid I'm missing it, staying in one place my whole life. What would you do if you were in my shoes?"

Alex shook his head. "That's the whole point, isn't it? Mor, I've seen some of the world, and for me, it just isn't the same as home. Tony still thinks I'm a fool for taking Hatteras West instead of the money when our folks died, but for me it was the only decision I could make. That lighthouse is a part of me. I could never leave it."

Mor nodded. The usual jocular tone of their talks was gone completely, replaced by a heaviness that hung in the air between them. "Don't get me wrong, Alex, you know I love Elkton Falls. But what I'm worried about is, will it be enough?"

"I wish I could answer that for you, Mor, I honestly do. I can tell you this. When I'm faced with a tough decision, I draw a line down the center of a sheet of paper, with pluses on one side and minuses on the other, just like Ben Franklin used to do. Sometimes I know the answer before I even finish my list. You might want to give it a try. It's worth a shot, anyway."

"I guess so." Mor looked back inside the small cottage. "Jase was just renting the place, wasn't he?"

"That's right. In fact, I have to move all his stuff out to Hatteras West in five days. Somebody's buying the cottage."

"You need a hand? With both our trucks, we should be able to make it in one trip."

Alex nodded. "That would be great." He paused a few seconds, then added seriously, "Mor, you need to do what's best for you, but if you decide to leave Elkton Falls, the place just won't be the same without you. I don't know what I'd do around here if you were gone."

Mor was about to answer when Sandra pulled up front in her BMW, parking behind Mor's truck.

"You two both look like you just lost your best friends in the world." She glanced at Alex a second, then said, "Sorry, that wasn't the best choice of words, was it?"

"Everything's fine here, Sandra," Alex said. "We were just taking a break."

She glanced at her watch. "Listen, if you two are in the middle of something, we don't have to go out tonight. Do you want a rain check on dinner, Alex? We can make it another time." She paused, then added, "I just had another thought. Mor, you're welcome to come along and join us."

The handyman stood and said, "No, thanks, but Alex would love to go; I can hear his stomach grumbling from here. I've got to get back to the shop."

Alex said, "Give me a call later, okay?"

Mor walked down the last porch steps as he said, "Sure thing. You two enjoy your dinner."

After Mor was gone, Alex said, "Just let me lock up, and I'll be ready to go." He searched his pockets for the keys but couldn't find them. "I'll be right back. I think I left the keys on the kitchen counter."

Alex found the keys in the bedroom and not in the kitchen where he'd expected to find them, then picked up the folder stuffed with papers from Jase's desk, the collectibles box, and the book he'd found on Jase's nightstand. Somehow he felt that it would help him hold onto his uncle a little longer, going through the last things in the world Jase had touched.

Irma Bean met them at the door of Mama Ravolini's with a raised eyebrow. "Two for dinner?"

Alex nodded, and as Irma led them to their table, she said, "So tell me, Alex, how is that wonderful Elise Danton you have working for you?"

"She's fine," he replied, trying to kill that particular conversation before it got started.

Irma wouldn't let up, though. "I hope you're treating her right. My, the way that woman can cook! What an asset she would be here in my kitchen."

Alex tried to hide his smile as he saw Sandra bite back a reply. Before she could get anything out, Alex said, "She's not leaving Hatteras West any time soon, Irma."

Irma patted him on the cheek as he sat down. "Good, that's where she belongs." Almost as an afterthought, Irma added, "You two enjoy your meal." As she started to walk away, she turned back to Alex and said, "Be sure to give her my love."

Alex agreed to do just that, then looked quickly at Sandra as Irma disappeared into the kitchen. She said, "That's all I need, an Elise Danton commercial."

Alex smiled as he said, "I don't think she means anything by it."

"Don't bet on it, Alex," Sandra said as she returned Alex's smile. "I think she means everything by it." She paused as their waiter immediately brought them two glasses of wine and a bottle of Alex's favorite, Chateau Morrisette's Sweet Mountain Laurel. It was from a vineyard in nearby Virginia, and Alex kept hoping to get a few days off to take a tour of the place someday. As the waiter poured, he said, "Compliments of the management."

The waiter added grandly, "Are you ready to order, or would you like some time with your menus?"

"I think we know what we want," Alex said as Sandra nodded her agreement. After they'd placed their orders, Sandra took a sip of wine, then said with a smile, "I don't need Irma Bean rubbing my nose in the fact that you've got a crush on Elise."

Alex protested, "She's engaged to someone else. In fact, I just found out her fiancé is moving to Elkton Falls to be closer to her."

Sandra took another sip of wine, then said, "Alex, Elise is never going to marry that man."

"Why do you say that?"

Sandra put down her glass and looked into his eyes. "If you ask me, she's just as interested in you as you are in her. Honestly, I wish you two would go out on a real date, just so you can get it out of your systems. This pining away isn't doing either of you any good."

Alex said awkwardly, "Sandra, you know Elise's presence didn't have anything to do with our breakup. We just—"

Sandra allowed herself a slight smile. "You don't even have to finish the sentence, Alex." She patted his hand as she added, "Our breakup was more my fault than it was yours. It was just that I saw so much potential in you, I knew you could do better than spending your life running an inn."

Before Alex could interrupt, she said, "Let me finish. Now I know that Hatteras West is where you belong. It's a part of you. I just wish it hadn't taken me so long to realize it." She took another sip of wine, then said, "To be honest with you, I'm kind of glad we're not dating anymore. I like you much better as a friend."

Alex lifted his glass, then paused. "I made my share of mistakes when we were dating, too." He moved his glass toward her. "Why don't we drink a toast, celebrating our friendship?"

Sandra nodded, and their glasses clinked together gently. "To friendship."

After a pleasant meal, Sandra drove Alex back to the inn, refusing a cup of coffee as a nightcap by pleading an early court date the next day.

Alex walked into the inn to find Elise sitting in the lobby by herself. There was a fire in the fireplace, and it seemed to him that it crackled with more sparks as he joined her.

Elise said, "Good, you're back. I've wanted to talk to you all day, but there never seems to be the chance." Her words tumbled out in a rush.

Alex leaned back in his chair as he placed the items he'd collected at Jase's on the table beside him. "How about now? I'm free if you are."

Elise took a deep breath, then said, "Alex, it's important for you to know that Peter came to Elkton Falls of his own accord. I did nothing to encourage him. In fact—"

"Elise, you don't have to explain anything to me. I know you've got a personal life of your own. That's allowed, you know," he said, trying to ease the sudden tension between them.

Elise twisted a hair tie in her hands. "You're more than just my boss, Alex; you're my friend. The thing is—"

She didn't get the chance to finish her sentence. Ashley Trask-Cooper took that moment to come downstairs. "Mr. Winston, there you are. I simply must have a word with you."

"In a minute," Alex said holding one hand up as he turned to Elise. "You were saying?"

"It can wait," Elise said as she stood abruptly.

"Elise, it had to be important, or you wouldn't have brought it up."

"Alex, we can talk later."

And before Alex could say another word, she was gone.

7

"What is it, Mrs. Cooper?" Alex said with little attempt to hide his ire. He was upset that his conversation with Elise had been so curtly interrupted.

The woman standing before him was obviously used to being treated with more diplomacy than Alex was showing, but she didn't let his abruptness faze her. Instead, a transformation much like her mother's came upon her. Ashley Trask-Cooper was suddenly quite charming as she said in a soft, friendly tone, "Alex, I know we've gotten off on the wrong foot, and I'd like to correct that right now. Call me Ashley; everyone else does. And I'll call you Alex, if you don't mind. It is Alex, isn't it?"

"That's right. So what can I do for you, Ashley?"

"Frankly, I'm worried about my brother. Have you seen him today?"

Alex said, "To be honest with you, I've been in and out most of the afternoon and evening. You might want to ask Elise if you're really concerned. She's been here at the inn all day."

Ashley shook her head. "I'm sure it's nothing. He's probably just blowing off some steam. He's certainly done it enough in the past. His moods can take such tortuous swings, and it's been a tough day for all of us."

Me, too, Alex added to himself. "I'm sure he's fine," Alex said aloud. At least Ashley's mother had possessed the decency to feign sympathy over Jase's death. Most likely Ashley was so wrapped up in her own little world that she didn't even notice that Alex had just lost someone dear to him.

Ashley touched his arm briefly, then offered him a slight smile as she said, "Thank you, I feel better just having spoken with you. I'm sure I'm just being silly. Good night, Alex."

"Good night," he said as she headed back up the stairs to her room.

Alex was used to a certain breed of guests who wanted to be on a first-name basis with the staff, trying to kid themselves that they really did believe all people were created equal. The truth was, he had a sneaking suspicion that what they really believed was that some were created just a little more equal than everyone else. To be fair, there was also the much more genuine type that wanted to be on a first name basis with the whole world, the people who didn't know any strangers; there were just friends they hadn't met yet. Mrs. Hurley, the home economics teacher who taught adult education classes at night, was one such person. She'd once been in a minor car accident while traveling in Texas, and by the time she'd been discharged from the hospital, she's made a dozen new friends who visited her regularly in Elkton Falls.

Alex ran into all types running the inn, and he was thankful that on the whole, his guests were a wonderful, friendly bunch who loved the lighthouse and grounds nearly as much as he did.

After Ashley was gone, Alex found himself wondering

for the hundredth time why Mathias Trask had insisted on
the Hatteras West Inn as the place for the reading of his
will. Alex had never heard of the man, and he'd spent most
of his life in Elkton Falls. Mathias must have moved away
when Alex's mother and father had been running Hatteras
West.

Most likely the man had fallen in love with the lighthouse as a boy and had wanted his family to share a last
moment with him there.

Alex could think of a whole host of worse wishes to
make.

The next morning, Alex and Elise worked together in
the laundry after cleaning the rooms. Since the loss of the
Dual Keepers' Quarters, they found things went smoother if
they worked together doing the daily chores that were involved in running an inn. Once the new building's construction was complete, they'd have to split up again to
make the most efficient use of their time, but for now, their
days were mostly spent together.

Nothing was said about their truncated conversation the
night before, and Alex knew he'd have to give Elise all the
time she needed to bring it up again. Though they'd never
gone out on a single date, Alex knew her better than he had
most of the girlfriends from his past.

As Elise transferred the last load of sheets from the
washer to the dryer, she said, "Alex, do you mind if I have
this evening off?"

"You're long past due for one. It's fine with me," he said
as he kept folding fresh towels he'd just taken from the
dryer.

Elise explained, "It's Peter. He wants us to have dinner
together tonight."

Alex said, "I'm sorry, I can't make it. Somebody's got to
stay here and run the inn." He saw the troubled look in her

eyes and added hastily, "I'm just kidding. Have a wonderful time."

Elise shut the door to the dryer as she said, "I'm sure we'll manage just fine."

After that, their conversation waned. Peter could manage that without even being there. He came between them like a wall, shutting everything else out. Alex didn't say anything else; he just kept folding towels in a quiet rhythm. It was remarkable how much laundry they did each and every day for just one building full of guests. At least it meant the inn was nearly full. It had to be, running as short on room space as they were. Even with complete occupancy, they were still in danger of dancing over into the red. Alex admitted that a healthy bequest of cash from Jase would have eased some of his more immediate worries about money, but he still took pride in the fact that his uncle had given him his most cherished possessions, probably because he knew full well that Alex would never sell a one of them. Tony, on the other hand, would have had an appraiser in looking over the books before sundown.

Elise finally spoke up. "Alex, are you all right?"

"I wish everyone would stop asking me that." He took a deep breath. "Don't worry, Elise, I'll be fine," he said, trying to act more together than he felt.

She stopped him from folding the towel in his hands and said, "I worry about you, Alex."

"I'm sorry if I'm not very good company right now, but I feel like I've just lost my father all over again. I've got to deal with it; I know that more than anyone else in the world, but it's hard."

She nodded gently. "I know it is, and I'm not helping matters, am I? Tell you what, why don't I cancel my plans with Peter tonight?"

"Don't, Elise, at least not on my account. I appreciate the offer, but I've got to get through this on my own."

"Okay, but I'm here if you need me," Elise said as she paused at the door.

Alex said, "I know that, and I greatly appreciate it. Believe me, I really do."

As he finished folding the towels, Alex pondered all that had gone on so recently. The loss of Jase, plus the added pressure of running an inn with too few rooms, was all starting to get to him.

Suddenly Alex felt some of the claustrophobia Mor had mentioned. If he was strictly honest with himself, at times he felt trapped by the responsibilities of running the inn. So why not take a few hours off? They were mostly caught up on their work, and what they hadn't done together, Elise could surely manage on her own. Since he was going to be inn-bound for the evening, there was time to go into town and see what he could learn about Jase's death. After telling Elise his plans, Alex got into his truck without a single glance back at the inn or the lighthouse above him as he headed into town.

Alex found Nadine Crowley working at her desk in Jase's office as if nothing had happened to the elder Winston. Then he saw the shredded tissue in one hand as she tried to file with the other. Jase Winston, a most conservative man, had obviously carried his tastes to his office more than his home, filling the law practice with somber emerald carpets, heavy woolen drapes and fine leather furniture.

"Hi, Mrs. Crowley . . . Nadine," he added quickly. She'd been his teacher in elementary school, and it had been nearly impossible to break the habit of calling her by her last name, no matter how much she insisted.

"Hello, Alex. I'm so sorry about your uncle. I know how close you two were."

Alex said, "Thanks. What are you going to do with yourself now?" Nadine's husband had dropped dead at her re-

tirement party a few years earlier, and she'd been forced to
go to work for a shady realtor. When he passed away as
well, Nadine had ended up working for Jase.

"I'm afraid to think about it right now. I haven't had
much luck working in the private sector. I may just face it
and retire in earnest."

Alex tried to buoy her with his words. "Come on, you've
got a lot still to contribute to the world. Don't give up
now."

She patted his hand. "You always were such a sweet boy.
Now, what brings you here, Alex? Oh, that's right. You've
inherited your uncle's possessions, haven't you?"

Alex said, "That's what Sandra said, but I'm not here to
take an inventory. I wanted to ask you about what happened
the other day."

Nadine selected a fresh tissue after discarding the shredded mess in her hand, then said, "Alex, I've been over this
a dozen times with Sheriff Armstrong. Must I go through it
all again with you?"

Alex said, "Of course not. I know you've been through a
lot. I won't add to your grief."

Nadine's gaze sharpened suddenly. "You're trying to
solve this yourself, aren't you?"

"To be honest with you, the thought had crossed my
mind. Nadine, Jase wasn't just my uncle; he was a lot more
than that to me."

Nadine nodded. "Alex, of course I'll help you. Jase was
a good man and the best boss I ever had. It's only fitting
that you try to find his killer." She stroked the edge of her
nose, thought for a few moments, then said, "Let's see, Jase
had the reading of the Trask will scheduled for later that
morning. As a general rule, your uncle didn't sleep in. He
was often here well before I started at eight A.M. every day.
I wish I could tell you what happened, but no one else was
here by the time I arrived." She started to cry but fought
back the tears as she added, "I don't think I'll ever be able

to forget how he looked just lying there with that lovely lighthouse you'd given him there beside him on the floor."

Alex realized how hard it must have been for Nadine to find Jase's body like that. He quickly switched tracks. "Nadine, tell me this. Why did Jase keep the Trask will in his safe? Was that normal procedure for him?"

Nadine said, "Heavens no, Alex, I'd never be able to find anything if he did that. No, Jase told me last week that the situation was a ticking time bomb, and that he'd better tuck the folder away where nobody could get their hands on it. Evidently it stood to shake things up quite a bit, but that's all he would say."

He nodded. "That explains why it was under such tight security."

"Oh, Alex, that's what's so tragic about it all. The thief didn't have to kill Jase; that safe hasn't worked in donkey years. All you have to do is wiggle the handle, and it opens right up. It was more of a hiding place than a safe. Jase was always meaning to get the safe repaired, but he used to claim that he never had anything valuable enough to store in it to justify the expense. I don't have to tell you that your uncle was a careful man with his money."

Alex tried to fight the impulse to say that Tony was reaping the benefits of that tendency now. He had to remember that he'd inherited exactly what Jase had wanted him to have.

"So who do you think killed him, Nadine?"

She looked down at her desk, shook her head and said, "I wish I knew, Alex, I truly do. I firmly believe you have to consider the Trask will as the catalyst in all of this, since it's the only thing I can find that's missing. Taking that into account, it could have been Trask's ex-wife or either of his children. It could have been Julie Hart, for that matter. The sheriff called a few minutes ago and had me check Jase's personal appointment book. Julie was scheduled for an appointment the night before he died, but I didn't know anything about it. Sheriff Armstrong is coming over here for the book."

Alex asked, "Was that unusual for Jase to add appointments to the schedule without telling you about it first?"

Nadine frowned. "As far as I can remember, it's never happened before. Our appointment books were usually identical."

"Could you check and see if there were any other odd entries you can't account for?"

"Of course. His book is still on his desk."

Alex followed Nadine into Jase's office. He could almost feel his uncle's presence in the room, with its overstuffed chairs and the walnut desk that stretched nearly across one side of the space.

She picked up a leather appointment book and opened it to the day before Jase died.

Her voice was sharp and immediate as she said, "Alex, this isn't right."

"What isn't?" Alex asked as he hurried to her.

"This notation for the appointment with Julie. It's not in Jase's handwriting. I knew there was something wrong about it before, but I couldn't put my finger on it."

Alex couldn't believe it. "So whoever killed Jase was trying to set Julie up?"

"It looks like it to me. I was so rushed when the sheriff called, but I can't believe I didn't spot it right away. What are we going to do about it?"

Alex studied the entry and said, "It's close enough to fool just about anybody. I can see how you missed it the first time you looked at it, Nadine. You need to point out the fact that the entry is a forgery when the sheriff gets here." Alex closed the leather-bound book and handed it to her.

Nadine said, "Alex, now that I know this is such an important clue, I can't stand the thought of it being here with me. What if something were to happen to it?"

"No one's going to come looking for it," Alex said. "Especially the forger. They want this appointment found, remember?"

"What if the killer gets cold feet and wants to retrieve the evidence? Alex, would you take it to the sheriff for me?"

He started to refuse the request, but one look at Nadine's face told him that she was honestly in fear for her safety. He reached for it and said, "Don't worry, I'll make sure he gets it."

Her relief was obvious. "Bless you, Alex."

As Alex tucked the appointment book under one arm, he added, "Do you have any idea where I can find Julie Hart?"

Nadine said, "From what I understand, her location is supposed to be a secret."

Alex said, "Nadine, you've known me all my life. I shouldn't have to assure you that I'm not going to hurt her."

Nadine studied him a moment, then said, "I know you're not, dear boy. She's staying with our resident sculptor, Amy Lang, but don't tell her I'm the one who told you."

"My lips are sealed. Thanks, Nadine, you've been a big help."

"Your uncle deserved a better ending than he got. I just hope you catch whoever did this, Alex."

"Me, too," Alex said as he headed out the door.

Stopping at the police station, Alex was told that the sheriff was at his usual hangout, Buck's Grill.

Sally Anne, Buck's daughter, met him with a forced smile.

Alex asked gently, "Hi, Sally Anne. How are you doing?"

"I'm better, Alex, thanks for asking. Dad's still in a stormy mood, though." Sally Anne's boyfriend had proposed to her, and three months later he'd broken their relationship off with her entirely. The two of them had been planning to hold the wedding at Hatteras West, with Alex's heartfelt approval. He loved it when the inn served as a chapel for local couples. His own parents had been married at the top of the lighthouse, and if Alex ever found someone of his own, he planned to do the same.

Alex found Sheriff Armstrong on a stool near the back, deep in conversation with Hiram Blankenship, his one-time rival for the sheriff's elected office. Hiram was the town barber, a man who had the unfortunate habit of waving his hands wildly in the air whenever he spoke. It wasn't so bad when Hiram held a sweet roll in his hand, but he could be frightening with a pair of scissors or a straight-edge razor slashing through the air.

"Hiram," the sheriff said, "what you don't know about the law could fill an ocean."

"I still say I would do a better job than you, you old goat," Hiram said, narrowly missing the sheriff's nose with a barrage of icing.

"The people of Elkton Falls didn't think so," Armstrong said as he leaned back on his stool to get out of harm's way.

"This time." Hiram gestured, stabbing at the sheriff with his roll. If it had been a sword, Elkton Falls would have needed a new sheriff after all. A smudge of icing stained the front part of Armstrong's uniform.

"You're going to pay for cleaning my uniform," Armstrong snapped as he pointed to the spot on his chest.

"The way you've been eating, who's going to notice one more stain?"

Alex knew he couldn't wait for the two men to wind down; they might be at each other the rest of the day. He said, "Sheriff, I need to talk to you."

Hiram snapped, "You're wasting your time, Alex, he's more interested in harassing taxpaying citizens than he is in solving crime."

Armstrong started to say something in reply when Alex added, "It's important."

The sheriff tried to tuck in his massive belly as he stood and faced Hiram. "If you'll excuse me, I've got police business to see to."

"There's no excuse for you," Hiram added just as they left the diner. Alex caught a broad grin on the barber's face as he managed to get the last jab in.

Armstrong said, "One of these days he's going to push me too far, Alex, you mark my words. Now what is it that's so all-fired important?"

Alex held the appointment book firmly in his hands. He wasn't ready to give it up until he made his point with Armstrong. "Nadine was too jumpy to keep this at the office."

The sheriff asked, "And how did you just happen to be there, Alex?"

"I inherited Jase's things, remember? I've got to start an inventory to see what I'm looking at." He had decided from the start not to let the sheriff know about his own investigation if he could help it.

"Sorry," Armstrong mumbled.

Alex said, "But since we're talking about the appointment book anyway, there's something you should know. Nadine swears the entry about Julie isn't in Jase's handwriting." Alex flipped the pages randomly and said, "See? She's right. None of the other entries match it, though it's pretty obvious somebody tried."

Armstrong picked right up on it. "So someone wanted to direct suspicion away from themselves, is that what you're thinking, that this is a frame-up?"

Alex nodded. "Exactly."

"I talked to Julie this morning," Armstrong admitted. "Of course, she denied ever making that appointment, but what would you expect her to say?"

Alex said, "But why would she forge her own name and not someone else's?"

"Hold on a second, Alex. What if Julie Hart is the real killer? She could have planted this to make it look like she was guilty at first, knowing the entry would never stand up in court."

Alex shook his head. "Sheriff, you've been watching too much television."

Armstrong bristled at the comment and grabbed the book. "First Hiram and now you! Alex, you need to leave the detecting to me. You've got an inn to run."

Alex knew from the tone of Armstrong's voice that he had overstepped his bounds, and he had to keep the sheriff's good will if he was going to get any information from him in the future.

"I guess you're right. Maybe I'd better get back to Hatteras West, then."

When the sheriff saw that Alex wasn't going to argue with him, he said kindly, "Alex, I'm sorry you lost your uncle. Believe me, I'm doing everything in my power to find the killer."

As Alex left, he nearly added, "So am I," but he kept that last remark to himself.

Alex had done as Nadine had requested and delivered the appointment book to the sheriff. It wasn't time to head back to Hatteras West yet, though. If he pushed it, he still had time to pay a visit to Julie Hart out at Amy Lang's homestead near Hatteras West. It was possible that there was something she wasn't telling him, and he was bound and determined to find out.

8

A creeping fog hugged the road as Alex drove up the lane to Amy Lang's homestead. It was an odd sight for early afternoon, but the weather had been strange lately as cold and warm fronts kept colliding over the foothills of the Blue Ridge Mountains. The gravel path was mostly obscured by the swirling masses of white, and Alex slowed his truck considerably as he drove.

Breaking out of the fog just ahead of him, an apparition appeared in a flash of red. Alex slammed on his brakes and stopped the truck. He'd come awfully close to hitting something!

"Why, if it isn't Alex Winston himself."

Amy Lang's jet-black hair tumbled out as she pulled back the hood of her bright red cloak.

"I could have killed you," Alex said, his voice shaking.

Amy laughed. "Nonsense. I knew where you were, even if you didn't see me. I was ready to jump if you got any closer."

Alex looked at her outfit and said, "I really like your cloak."

She twirled in it, and the material danced elegantly around her with a few wisps of swirling fog dancing in rhythm. Amy said, "It's an Irish walking cape. Stunning, isn't it?"

Alex laughed gently. "You're doing everything in your power to keep the eccentric artist myth alive, aren't you?"

She smiled. "What can I say? It lets me keep my prices up." The banter subsided as Amy asked, "What brings you out this way? I know you're too busy with the inn to just pop in unannounced."

Alex said, "Let me get my truck off the road first. I don't want to get rear-ended. Would you like a ride back to your place?"

"You didn't answer my question."

Alex knew Amy well enough to realize that she wasn't going to budge until he answered her. "I need to speak with Julie Hart."

"And what makes you think she's out here?"

Alex said, "I've got to protect my sources. So, can I see her?"

"It all depends, Alex. Are you going to harass her, too?"

"I just want to talk," Alex said. "Please, it's important."

Another figure stepped out of the mist wearing a cape done in blue instead of Amy's red.

"It's okay, Amy, Alex and I have already met. I'd like to think we're friends."

Amy turned to Julie. "You know what Sandra said; you shouldn't be talking to anyone right now."

Alex said, "Amy, we don't know each other all that well, but if you'd like to go into town and ask around, I guarantee you'll find out that I don't take advantage of people. I'll come back out after you two have decided whether I'm trustworthy or not."

As he headed back to his truck, Julie said, "We don't need to check your references, Alex. I trust you."

Amy said, "I do, too. It's just that you've got a lot at stake, Julie."

Julie laughed. "I came here with nothing, and if I leave that way, there's no real change in my life, now is there?"

Amy said, "That's fine. It's your decision. Listen, I'm walking back to the studio. I have to finish that sculpture for Clarion Industries."

Alex said, "Ladies, I'd be glad to give you both a lift back."

"And miss this fog? It's a lot more fun walking," Amy said.

Julie interjected, "I don't mind riding, Amy. It'll give us a chance to talk."

Amy said, "Suit yourself then," as she disappeared back into the mist, pulling the hood up as she vanished from sight.

Alex held the door open for Julie as she slid onto the seat. "Have you two known each other long?" he asked.

"Since college. We were roommates our freshman year. I was kind of surprised when that letter from your uncle came mentioning Elkton Falls. I'd been planning to visit Amy all along." Julie turned in her seat and looked at Alex. "Listen, I'm sorry you've wasted a trip out here. I've decided to withdraw my claim on the estate. It's just not worth it to me emotionally. If I'd known Mathias, even met him once, I might feel differently about it all, but I just can't fight with his family for something I'm not all that sure I deserve. Honestly, I just want to get out of Elkton Falls and never come back."

Alex said, "Don't you think your father's wishes should be honored?"

Julie said, "My father? I've been thinking about that a lot lately, Alex. I can't see that Mathias had any right to make that claim on his deathbed; he was never there for me when he was alive, not once in all those years."

It was a point Alex couldn't argue. He and his own father, though they'd gone through some rocky times in their relationship, had carried a strong bond between them that went well beyond a mutual love for their lighthouse in the mountains.

Alex decided it was time to bring Julie up to speed on the latest developments in town. After telling her about the forgery in Jase's appointment book, he said, "You realize you're a suspect in Jase's murder, don't you? How is it going to look if you just take off? Armstrong's not going to like it."

The idea was obviously something Julie hadn't considered. "Oh, Alex, I could never have killed your uncle. We never met, but the time I spoke with him on the telephone, he was extremely nice to me. How can anyone think I could do such a thing?"

"That listing in Jase's appointment book the night before he was killed looks bad to Armstrong."

Julie said, "I gathered as much from what the sheriff said when he came out here this morning, but I swear, I never had an appointment with him, that day or any other."

Alex nodded. "I believe you. Jase's secretary and I compared the handwriting, and someone besides Jase put your name in that book. It looks like someone's trying to frame you for murder. You must be a real threat. Don't you see that?"

"It just doesn't make sense," Julie said as Alex crept down the lane.

He took a deep breath, then said, "I know this isn't what you want to hear, but I'm going to say it anyway. Julie, shouldn't you consider the possibility that you *do* have a stake in all this? Mathias asked you to come here to meet the rest of his family, your family, when it comes right down to it. I'm not making excuses for his abandoning you, but it does look like he truly wanted you to share in his wealth. I don't think it's just about the money though, or he could have sent you a check and been done with it.

Wouldn't you like to have a connection with someone you're related to by blood? Isn't it worth another try?"

They rode in silence a few minutes until Alex's headlights picked up Amy's welding shop and studio through the breaking fog, a converted barn that had once housed cattle. Alex turned off the engine but made no move to get out.

Julie finally said, "You know, maybe you're right. Alex, Mathias Trask thought of me as his daughter, and he wanted me to have a share of his family and his estate. It would be wrong of me to deny him his final wish."

Alex nodded, then tried to get out fast enough to open Julie's door, but she beat him to it.

Amy came out of the mist behind them, the hood of her cape still pulled up. As she pushed it back, she said, "Is everything all right?"

Alex was about to say something when Julie chimed in, "Everything's just fine. We're finished with our little talk."

Alex wanted to ask a few more questions, but the firmness in Julie's voice was hard to contradict. "For now, at least."

Amy said brightly, "Enough talk about the dark things then. Come see what I'm doing," she added as she led them to the barn doors and flung them open.

Inside, sitting on a turntable pedestal in the middle of the barn, was a towering sculpture that at first looked like an odd collection of junk. As Alex studied it, though, he could make out the form of a body inside the twists of steel. A projection that had at first appeared to be tacked on became a hand reaching upward, and once he found that in the steel, he saw the face gazing up as well.

Amy looked at it a moment, then asked, "So what do you think I should call it?"

Alex studied it for a few seconds more, then said, "How about *Reaching for the Stars*?"

Amy shrugged as Julie applauded and said, "What a

great name, but she's calling it *Exceeding Dreams*. I've got to admit, it's kind of growing on me."

Amy said, "Hey, I don't name them, they tell me what they should be called."

Alex said, "I'll have to trust you on that. Listen, I'd better get back to the inn. Elise has been covering the place for me all day."

Julie said, "Couldn't you at least stay for a bite to eat? We're just having sandwiches, but you're more than welcome to join us."

Alex was tempted, but he was also leery of leaving Elise too long at the inn alone. "Thanks, but I'd better get back. How about a rain check?"

Amy nodded, her thoughts already back to the steel.

Julie walked him out, staying close to him as they neared the truck. As he got in, she said, "You have a real positive energy, Alex. I like it."

"Thank you kindly, ma'am. I'd like to talk more later, if that's all right with you."

"I'd be delighted," she said, and he drove off into the fog.

Though the two properties were within a few miles of each other by the map, the roads he needed to take him back home would take at least twenty minutes, especially in the fog. Alex wondered about Julie's change of heart as he headed back to Hatteras West. Had she truly decided to give up her inheritance before Alex spoke with her, or had it all been for his benefit? He liked Julie, there was no doubt about that, but could he believe her?

He still hadn't made up his mind as he pulled up the long lane of Point Road that led to the lighthouse's front door.

Alex's heart fell when he saw a shiny new BMW parked out front. He'd half wished it was Sandra's or even Tony's, but he should have been so lucky.

It appeared that Peter Asheford had made good his threat to come to Elkton Falls.

Steeling himself, Alex parked his truck and walked inside.

Peter and Elise were sitting by the fireplace in deep conversation when Alex walked in. They both stood as he approached, Peter sticking by her side.

Elise said, "Alex, if you don't mind, we're going to go ahead and take off early."

Nodding to Elise without really looking at her, Alex looked in Peter's direction as he said, "Absolutely. Thanks for hanging around."

Peter walked forward and offered his hand to Alex. "Good to see you again. The last time I was here, your other building was burned to the ground. Fantastic start at the reconstruction job. Elise gave me the grand tour."

Alex took Peter's hand, fighting his instinct to warm to the man. Peter Asheford was a natural-born salesman, no matter what else he might be.

Alex said, "Thanks. I'm really proud of it."

"As you should be." Peter lowered his eyes as he added, "Sorry to hear about your uncle. I hope there won't be any bad feelings between us."

"Why on earth should there be?" Alex asked.

Peter said, "I had no idea when I bought the cottage that it belonged to your uncle. I just don't want you to think I'm taking advantage of your tragedy."

Alex knew someone had bought his uncle's rental cottage, but he'd had no idea it was Elise's fiancé behind his eviction. That was no way to look at it; Jase was done with the house forever. "It's a great place. I'll have his things cleared out by tomorrow night."

Peter shook his head. "Nonsense. There's no hurry; I plan to be here a long time."

Elise glanced at her watch and said, "We really need to go."

Peter nodded, then said, "Good afternoon, Alex."

"See you later," he said as he watched them walk away.

So that was that. Peter Asheford had made his intentions quite clear. Elkton Falls had just gained a new resident, and at the same time witnessed the dying of a dream. If there had been any doubt in his mind before, Alex now knew that there was no way he could compete with this man for Elise's heart, not when it appeared that Peter Asheford already claimed it.

It was, sadly, time to move on.

After they were gone, Alex went into his office to clear some of the paperwork he'd been neglecting lately. It seemed as though there was always a bill to pay or a letter that had to be answered. A great many people thought it was some elaborate joke when they heard about the lighthouse in the mountains, so Alex had to assure them of the fact that Hatteras West was indeed run as an inn where they could stay.

Alex's stomach rumbled as he continued through the pile of mail. Paperwork could eat up more of his day than his guests sometimes. When Alex glanced at the clock, he saw that it was nearly time to eat dinner. He was just finishing up a letter to a woman in Wilmington named Susan in need of assurance that the inn in fact truly existed, when the front door of the inn banged open. It was Steven Trask, and from the look on his face, he was frantic about something as he stumbled in.

Alex jumped up from his desk. "What's wrong?"

Steven said, "I was out walking the grounds, and I swear someone was following me! When I called out to them, they wouldn't answer. I ran all the way back here. Someone's stalking me!"

"I'm sure it's nothing as serious as all that," Alex said, trying to soothe the man. "The woods around here can play strange tricks on you, especially at dusk." Most likely it was a squirrel or some other small forest animal skittering about on the trails. Steven had *city boy* written all over him.

"I'm telling you, someone was following me!"

Alex thought about it a second, then asked, "Is it possible it might have been our groundskeeper? If you're not expecting him, Vernum can be a little startling, but I can assure you, he's harmless."

Steven wasn't buying it. "I'm not imagining things, and I'm not talking about someone on your staff. This was an intentional attempt at rattling me! Now are you going to call the sheriff, or am I going to have to do it myself?"

Alex said, "Just hold on a second. How about this? Why don't I go check it out myself." He reached behind the desk and pulled out a large flashlight.

"You're actually going to go out there alone?"

Alex nodded. "I was raised here. Don't worry about me; I'll be fine."

Steven looked at him in disbelief, then said, "I personally think you're insane, but be my guest. Be warned, though. If you're not back in ten minutes, I'm calling 911."

Alex said, "Give me at least thirty minutes before you do anything like that."

Steven said reluctantly, "We'll make it twenty. I'm not normally so jumpy, but I'm telling you, Alex, somebody's out there, and they're up to no good."

Alex saw real fear in Steven's eyes. Could he be right? Was there someone stalking a guest at the inn? And could it possibly have anything to do with Jase's murder?

There was only one way to find out. Clutching the flashlight a little tighter than he needed to, Alex walked out the front door into the growing night.

9

"Hello? Is anybody out there?"

Alex called out into the darkness, not expecting a response, but he heard something crashing through the woods ahead of him. From the sound of the footsteps, it was a little too big for a chipmunk or a squirrel.

When he flashed the light in the direction of the sound, though, there was nothing there. At least nothing he could see. There hadn't been a bear sighted in Elkton Falls for ten years, not since the last big drought had driven one down from the mountains in search of food, but they hadn't had much rain lately, and Alex couldn't help wondering if one might be around now. His imagination was taking over full throttle, and every shape and shadow around him was assuming the guise of a killer bear or a deranged murderer lurking in wait for him.

"Stop it, Alex. You know better," he chided himself out loud. The sound of his voice helped calm him, and the ominous shapes he'd seen for a moment converted back into trees, bushes, and a lawn chair someone had left out in the woods.

He made the rest of the rounds of the property with a lighter heart after he'd banished the demons from his mind. After circling the path from Bear Rocks to both inn buildings to the lighthouse itself, Alex was satisfied that there was no one or nothing ominous out there. At least not now.

Alex stopped at the storage shed by the lighthouse to check on Vernum. Perhaps the man had been wandering around the woods on his own, oblivious to the fact that he'd startled one of Alex's guests. Inside the shed, he found that the cot was still made up, but the arborist was nowhere to be found. Alex saw an odd-looking stamp on the floor and a pile of old magazines spread out on the bed. The collection was so odd, it had to have come from Les Williamson's collection. Mor's partner had the most eclectic taste in all of Canawba County. *Could* Vernum have been the one walking out in the woods? If he had, why hadn't he identified himself when Steven had called out to him? That was a question he wouldn't have to ask. Vernum was notoriously shy, and Alex doubted he would respond to any hail or summons coming from a stranger.

In the morning, Alex promised himself that the two of them would have a long talk, even if Alex had to sit on him to make Vernum stay in one place long enough for more than three words! The man's shyness was astounding!

He was still smiling at the image of pinning Vernum down for their dialogue when he walked back into the inn. Steven was at the desk with one hand on the telephone, poised to pounce on the numbers.

"Did you see anything? Was he still out there?"

"Whoever or whatever it was is long gone now," Alex said as he switched off his flashlight.

"Somebody was out there in the woods. You've got to believe me, Alex; I'm telling the truth."

Alex said, "I believe you," as sincerely as he could muster. "Most likely it was just my landscaper. Vernum is extremely shy; I doubt he'd answer his own mother if she called him."

"And if it wasn't him?" Steven pressed.

Alex said, "Sometimes people from town come out here and run the trails at night."

"In the dark? And why didn't they identify themselves when I called out?"

"They could have had headphones on, or be lost in their own thoughts. I'm certain there's a logical explanation for it, Steven."

The young man shook his head. "I'm still not leaving the inn by myself after dark from here on out."

"I understand completely."

Steven moved to the stairs, then paused and said, "I understand there's going to be a wake for your uncle here tomorrow night. I'll do my best to get my sister and mother out of the inn so you can have some time alone to grieve."

Alex was touched by the gesture. "You are all invited, Steven. It's going to be a celebration of his life. That's the way he wanted it. You never got the chance to meet Jase, but I can tell you, he embraced the world. I'm sure he would have invited you all himself, if he could have. Jase always was one who believed the more the merrier."

Steven looked uncomfortable. "But still, I can't help feeling we are somewhat responsible. After all, it was Father's will that led to his death. How can we show our faces at the man's wake?"

"You can't blame yourself," Alex said, adding to himself, *Unless you're the one who killed him.*

Steven looked as if he was about to say something else when his sister came down the stairs. "I thought I heard your voice. Steven Trask, where have you been?"

"Ashley, I needed to get away for awhile."

She said, "The next time you feel the urge to just walk off, tell me where you're going first. I was worried sick about you."

Steven replied, "I guess there's a first for everything, isn't there?" He turned back to Alex and said, "Good night, and thanks for your kind offer."

"Good night," Alex said.

He was surprised when Ashley didn't follow her brother up the stairs. Instead, she walked down and joined him near the desk. If she was indeed so worried about Steven, why hadn't she followed him back to his room?

It was clear there was something on her mind, but Alex wasn't sure he cared what it was at that moment. It had been a long day, and tomorrow would come early enough.

He said, "Well, if you'll excuse me, I'll say good night now."

She touched his arm lightly. "Alex, I'm concerned about Steven. He hasn't been acting irrationally around you, has he?"

"What do you mean?"

Ashley said, "I'm afraid he's going to hurt himself. He's been depressed lately, and with your uncle's death, I'm afraid it's pushing him off the deep end."

Alex said, "He seems fine to me."

Ashley nodded, then said, "Steven's a master at disguising how he feels, but believe me, he's in real pain. I just wish he would listen to me and get help before it's too late."

"You're that concerned about him? What does your mother think?"

Ashley shook her head. "Mother has a bit of tunnel vision when it comes to her youngest. She thinks the sun rises and sets by her precious baby boy."

"I don't know what to tell you, Ashley. If there's anything I can do, let me know."

She touched his arm lightly. "Thanks, Alex, I'll do that. Just keep an eye on him, could you do that for me please?"

Alex stifled a yawn, then said, "I'll do what I can. Now, if you'll excuse me, it's been a long day."

"Forgive me for keeping you up, Alex. Do you mind if I go through your bookshelves and find something to read? I can't fall asleep without reading."

He said, "Help yourself. I've got everything from poetry to mysteries to short story anthologies to history to biographies."

She smiled. "Surely I'll be able to find something with all that available. Good night, Alex. And thanks. I feel better just talking to someone about my brother."

"Happy to help."

As Alex got ready for bed, he wondered if it could be true that Steven was so depressed. The man hadn't acted like it since he'd been at the inn, but what did that prove? Alex knew it could go well beyond the surface, and Ashley did seem genuinely concerned about her brother. Should he keep an eye on Steven, try to make sure he didn't do anything rash? No, as much as Alex would like to think that he was lord and master of the Hatteras West Inn, he knew that he couldn't protect everyone there, especially from themselves. All he could do was be the best host he could, giving his guests every opportunity to have an enjoyable time at the inn. After that, it was up to them.

Alex took out the three items he'd brought with him from Jase's house. Putting the box aside for a moment, Alex leafed through the papers tucked neatly in Jase's folder, wondering if there was some clue to the man's death hidden inside. There were bills, neatly organized by when payments were due, a few credit card receipts, and a handful of letters waiting to be answered, but no sign of any legal documents at all. Alex grew excited as he skimmed through the envelopes, hoping to find one with a torn flap, but all had been neatly slit open with a letter opener. From a quick glance at the contents, there was nothing of interest there, and Alex felt like a voyeur going through his uncle's

personal papers. Alex picked up the book he'd taken off
Jase's nightstand, opened it to the introduction and started
to read. His gaze kept drifting back to the collectibles box,
and Alex could resist the temptation no more. He spread
out his uncle's treasures on the bed in front of him, finding
a few new stones he'd never seen before, a tie clip with a
chip of gold embedded in it and a folded note at the bottom
of the box.

It startled him to find his own name printed on the front
of the paper, and with trembling hands, he opened it. It was
short, simple, and to the point. In Jase's handwriting, it
said, "Alex, enjoy these as I have. My treasures are now
yours. Jase."

A soft sob escaped Alex's lips as he folded the note back
up and returned it to the bottom of the box. It was too soon
to take it all in. Alex put the collection back in the box, then
slid it, along with the books and the folder, under the edge
of his bed. He was too tired to find a spot for them on his
crowded nightstand tonight.

Just before he turned out the light, Alex glanced at the
clock by his bed and saw that it was nearing midnight.
There was no sign of Elise and Peter. He was still wondering what that meant as he drifted off to sleep.

"Hey, Alex, got a second?"

Alex had been signing checks and paying bills the following morning, and any interruption was a welcome one.

Even from his brother.

"Come on in, Tony," he said as he closed his checkbook.
There was no way he wanted his brother to see the details
of his finances.

Tony sat across from him and said, "Listen, I've been
feeling a little guilty about the way this has all played out.
Jase was wrong to give me all that money. I'd like you to at
least have some of it."

Alex shook his head. "I appreciate the offer, but I'll have to pass."

"You're too proud for your own good, Alex." Tony took a deep breath, then said, "Listen, I grew up here, too. I know what it takes to run this place. You're just barely scraping by; don't try to deny it."

Alex said, "I'm doing well enough. You don't understand, Tony, it's truly not a matter of pride." Alex paused a second, then added, "Well, not entirely. The thing is, I'm getting exactly what Jase wanted me to have; no more, no less."

"You're as stubborn as Dad ever was," Tony said in disgust.

"Said the kettle to the pot," Alex answered with a smile.

Tony laughed. "Yeah, I guess you've got me there. Okay, let's forget we ever had this conversation."

"Are you kidding? My brother offers to part with some of his money, and you expect me to forget it? Not on your life."

Tony nodded, then said seriously, "Alex, I thought I should let you know, I'm leaving tomorrow morning. This place," he gestured with a sweep of his hand to take in all of Hatteras West, "it just doesn't have anything for me anymore."

Alex admitted, "I didn't figure I'd ever see you back here again."

Tony shrugged. "You were the one in love with the lighthouse, not me. I outgrew Elkton Falls a long time ago, and this place, too."

"I'm sorry you feel that way," Alex said softly.

"Hey, no offense intended," Tony said.

"None taken. We chose different paths, that's all."

Tony stood and stretched. "Well, I just wanted to clear that up."

"Consider it done," Alex said as he watched his brother leave. The offer of sharing Jase's money had startled Alex, truth be told. Maybe he'd been wrong about his brother. Perhaps Tony had grown some in the years since they'd talked last.

There was a knock on the door, and Mor walked in. "Is this a bad time?"

"There don't seem to be many good ones lately, so come on in," Alex said.

Mor started to edge out of the office. "We'll catch up later."

Alex stood. "Listen, I'm sorry. I'm just having a hard time with all that's been going on around here the past few days."

Mor said, "I just came by to see if you wanted to go get Jase's stuff, but we can do it another time."

Alex looked at the latest bills still to pay, then said, "Now's as good a time as any. Let me tell Elise, then we can go."

Alex found Elise starting her rounds upstairs. "I need an hour or two in town. Can you cover here?"

Elise said, "Absolutely. Are you getting things set up for tonight?"

"No, Jase took care of all the arrangements before he died. It's weird, almost as if he knew something was going to happen."

Elise said, "Alex, he wasn't a young man."

"He was still too young to die," Alex replied.

"I didn't mean anything by it, Alex, just that he wanted to be ready."

Alex nodded. "Yeah, I guess you're right. Listen, if you need me for anything, Mor's going to help me pack up Jase's things at his cottage."

Elise said, "I wish I could help, but somebody has to be here for our guests."

"Thanks anyway," he said as he left her in the hallway.

Downstairs, Mor asked, "Is everything okay?"

"No, but it will be," Alex said as they walked out of Hatteras West.

10

"So how's your life going?" Alex asked Mor as they loaded up another box of books. "Have you made up your mind about what you're going to do with Les's offer?"

"Not yet," Mor said. With a grin, he added, "I'm kind of hoping if I put it off long enough, Les will change his mind."

"Any chance of that happening?"

Mor shook his head. "I don't think so. The man's in love. He's leaving, and I'm tired of trying to convince him to stay." Mor taped up the box he was working on, then picked it up. Alex grabbed another box, and the two men walked out to Mor's truck. Alex had wondered if he should have brought his truck as well, but Mor convinced him that they could get everything into the back of his long-bed pickup.

Sadly, it looked like there was going to be room left over.

Mor said, "How are you holding up?"

"It's tough, I won't deny it, but I'm finally starting to accept the fact that Jase is gone."

Mor nodded. "Elise's fiancé picked a bang-up time to come to town, didn't he? That can't be helping matters."

Alex said stiffly, "It's none of my business. I figured he'd be here sooner or later."

"Come on, Alex, this is your old buddy you're talking to. I know it's killing you to see her with somebody else."

Alex said, "I'll get over it. She made her choice a long time ago, and I'm just going to have to live with it."

"Did she, though? Elise didn't know you when she said yes to him."

Alex said, "I've got to face facts and get on with my life. Elise and I just weren't meant to be."

As the two men walked back inside, Mor nodded as he surveyed the cottage's small rooms. "That looks to be the last of Jase's personal stuff in here. Alex, should we head over to the law office and do the job right, or do you want to save it for another day?"

"Let's just get it over with. If you don't mind, why don't you go ahead and get in the truck? I'll be out in a bit. I just need a minute or two alone."

"Take your time," Mor said. "I decided to take the whole morning off. I figure I won't get the chance after Les retires. If I buy him out, that is."

After his friend was gone, Alex walked around the cottage alone, trying to capture the last essence of his uncle there. It was odd, but with the books gone and Jase's clothes sent off to the Salvation Army, the place was just an empty shell, not the home Jase had made for himself. There was nothing of the man left there. Alex wasn't sure what he'd been expecting, but there was no trace of Jase's quick laugh or his bright smile in the walls around him. The essence of his uncle, what made him special, was long gone in one sense, and in another very real way buried deep in Alex's heart.

There was nothing left behind to savor, to grasp, to love.

Peter was welcome to all that was left behind.

•   •   •

It was quick work packing the few personal things of Jase's in his office. Sandra had agreed to take care of the law books and his pending files, a dealer was taking all the furniture on consignment, and what little was left fit into three packing boxes.

Nadine hovered over them as they worked. As Mor carried a box downstairs, Alex finished packing up the last bits of his uncle's life and found the companion book to *The Treasure Below, Treasure in the Hills,* on his desktop. Alex added it to his stack as Nadine said, "I swear I meant to do this myself. I just didn't realize you'd want it done so quickly."

Alex said, "I don't mind, Nadine. I hope you don't take this the wrong way, but I'm surprised you're still here. I can't pay you anything for your work. I wish I could."

Nadine said, "Your brother's taken care of it till the end of the week, Alex. He said it was the least he could do."

Alex nodded. So Tony had done the right thing after all. "That was good of him. You know I would have done it myself, but . . ."

Nadine touched his shoulder lightly. "Alex, you don't have to explain anything to me. I knew what Jase was going to do, though I tried to talk him out of it till I was blue in the face. He said his books would mean more to you than any stocks or bonds ever could. I'm afraid he might have seen your construction out there as a sign that you were doing well enough on your own financially." She paused, then said, "You know how worried he was about your brother."

"No, I didn't know anything about that. What are you talking about, Nadine?"

She looked flustered. "Oh, dear. I'm afraid I've already said too much."

Alex wasn't about to let it go that easily. "Not enough, in my opinion. What's going on?"

"Alex, I really shouldn't say."

He was in no mood for games. "Then I'll just have to ask Tony myself."

"No, you can't do that," she pleaded.

"One way or the other, I'm going to find out."

Nadine nodded. "I know you, Alex, you're like a dog with an old bone when you're trying to get to the truth about something. All right, I'll tell you, but you must swear never to let your brother know you're aware of his situation. Tony's in trouble financially. He came to Jase a few months ago and asked him for a loan. Your uncle gave him something, but Tony kept saying it wasn't enough. I didn't mean to eavesdrop, but the two of them had words. The walls here aren't that thick."

"Why didn't he come to me if he was in trouble?"

"Alex, Tony knew you couldn't give him the kind of help he needed. From what I gathered before, Jase's inheritance will just barely get him out of trouble. That's why he got so much of the stock." She looked as if she was going to cry. "Oh Alex, please don't tell him I told you about this. Your brother has a lot of pride, more than is good for him, I'll wager."

"I won't say a word," Alex promised.

Nadine said, "I've got to get some fresh air," as she dabbed at her cheeks. "If you wouldn't mind, could you lock up when you leave?"

As soon as Alex was alone, he walked to the safe where Jase's body was found. There was no chalk outline on the floor, just a single stain on the carpet where he'd died.

A horrible thought suddenly struck Alex.

What if they were all on the wrong track about Jase's murder?

What if Mathias's will wasn't the real reason Jase had been killed? Was it possible, the unthinkable thought floating around in his mind? Could Jase's murder have been committed because of greed closer to home? He couldn't imagine Tony actually murdering their uncle, but Nadine had said he was in dire financial trouble, and people had killed for a lot less than a hundred thousand dollars.

As much as he hated to admit it, Alex realized that if he looked at his uncle's murder objectively, Tony had to be considered a suspect.

"Hey Alex, are you all right?"

Alex looked up from the box he'd been staring at to find Mor a few feet away. He'd been so lost in his thoughts that he hadn't even heard his friend come back in. "Sorry, I must have zoned out."

"You're entitled to, buddy. This has got to be hard for you." Mor looked around the room. "So what happens to all this? Do we pack it all?"

"Sandra's handling the cases Jase was working on, except where they were going against each other, so she's getting a lot of the files. A lawyer from Hickory's coming over to handle the rest. He hinted to Sandra that he might be interested in buying the entire practice."

"So you might see something out of this after all?" Mor asked.

"From all accounts, there's not much to buy. Jase ran this law office as a hobby more than anything else. I'm glad he did; he was happiest when he was working on a case. I've got his personal books. That's all I care about."

Mor said, "I understand how you feel, but you've got to be pragmatic, too. I know what Hatteras West costs you to operate. If this guy makes an offer, I'd get what I could out of it."

"We'll worry about that when the time comes." He looked around once more, then said, "Let's go. There's nothing else here for me."

As they stowed the last box in the truck, Mor said, "Well, that's one way to burn a morning. Let's go over to Buck's and grab some lunch."

Alex said, "I don't know if I should. I've left Elise alone all morning."

"So what's another half hour going to hurt?" Mor hesitated, then said, "Tell you what, I'll even buy. You're not going to get a better deal than that. What do you say?"

"I say we go before you change your mind," Alex said. "Why don't we walk over? It's a pretty day, and I could use the fresh air."

"Why not," Mor agreed, so they headed over to Buck's on foot.

Buck's Grill was jammed, nearly overflowing with the noonday crowd. Sally Anne, Buck's daughter, barely had time to nod toward them as she hustled past with a tray heavily loaded with food.

Irene Wilkins, the beautician/criminologist, called them over to her booth. "Would you two gentlemen care to share a table with me? It's the only way you'll eat sitting down today."

Alex slid in beside her and said, "Now how can we turn down such a gracious offer? But Irene, are you sure your reputation can handle being seen with the two of us?"

Mor winked at her as he added, "I'm not sure anyone's name could survive that particular blow. Just don't tell Emma about this when she gets back. She has a tendency to get jealous when I pay too much attention to another woman."

Irene laughed heartily, catching the other diners' attention for a moment before they went back to their discussions. Though the food was good enough, Alex believed most of the customers were there as much for the conversation as they were for the meal.

Irene asked, "So how's life at the inn, Alex?"

"Never a dull moment. We're trying to get everything ready for tonight." He glanced at his watch. "In fact, I should be there right now, but Mor offered to buy lunch, and I wasn't about to pass that up."

Mor said, "Keep your voice down, will you? I have a reputation to uphold." He glanced at the crowd and said, "Tell you what, why don't I go ahead and order for us at the counter? Sally Anne's really hopping, and I'm hungry enough to eat a moose."

"How do you know what I want?" Alex asked.

"Come on, anybody in Elkton Falls could order for you, Alex. Club sandwich, no tomato, fries, and iced tea. Now tell me I'm wrong."

"You're wrong," Alex said. "Since you're buying, I think I'll start with the filet mignon, maybe a chocolate mousse and a bottle of Buck's finest champagne."

Mor laughed. "Right. I'll go place that order right away, sir."

After he was gone, Irene said somberly, "Alex, there's something I've been wanting to talk to you about, but I didn't know how to go about it."

"Is it about my uncle?" Alex asked.

"Yes, but not in the way you think. It's . . . well . . . it's all rather personal."

Alex said, "I swear I won't breathe a word. What are you holding back?"

Irene lowered her voice. "It's not about the case, Alex. Jase and I, well, we were friends. I don't know if you've heard, but we had a habit of sharing our Thursday evenings together. He'd come over and I'd cook us a big meal, then we'd sit in the parlor and play a few games of chess." Irene said, "Don't look so surprised. Beauticians can play chess, too."

"It's not that. I know you're one of the smartest folks in Elkton Falls. I just didn't realize you were dating my uncle."

Alex had to look hard to believe what he was seeing. The

unflappable Irene was actually blushing! "Oh, I wouldn't go that far. We simply enjoyed each other's company."

Alex touched her hand lightly. "Irene, you were crying when the sheriff and I came by your shop the other day, and here I thought it was just the chemicals. Listen to me. If you gave Jase some companionship in his last days, I couldn't be happier. I'm just amazed you managed to keep it a secret. I thought the kudzu vine was impossible to beat."

"Well, Jase was a crafty old rascal. He had a real knack for keeping his private life private, if you know what I mean."

Alex said softly, "And no one in town knows you're grieving, Irene. I'm so sorry for your loss," he said as he gently patted her hand.

Tears welled up in Irene's eye. "Alex Winston, you are the sweetest man I know. I should be the one offering words of comfort to you."

Mor came back and slid an iced tea in front of Alex, with another for himself. He said, "Your steak will be right up, sir, but they were all out of champagne. Anything else from the bar while you're waiting?"

It took Mor a second to realize he'd interrupted something. "I just remembered, I have a call to make, if you two will excuse me."

Irene put a hand on his arm. "You're not going anywhere until you sit down and tell me your plans."

"What plans are those?"

"Mor Pendleton, I've been running To Dye For nearly twenty-seven years. Do you think there's a chance in the world I haven't heard what Les has done?"

Mor said, "Now, why am I not surprised?" Mor looked at his tea, swirled the glass a few times without taking a sip, then said, "To be honest with you, I haven't decided yet."

Irene said softly, "Elkton Falls needs you, Mordecai Pendleton. Don't leave us."

The big man was obviously uncomfortable by the serious turn of the conversation. "Don't worry, you're not going to get rid of me any time soon."

Alex said, "Irene, we'll see you at the inn tonight for the send-off, won't we?"

"I don't know, Alex, I' m not sure—"

"Nonsense," Alex said. "I want you there as my personal guest. I'm sure it's what Jase would have wanted."

Irene said, "I'll be there, then." She threw a twenty on the table over her bill. "Lunch is on me, gentlemen," Irene said as she rushed out of Buck's before the men could say another word.

"Alex, my friend, your way with women is unparalleled in the history of all mankind."

"What can I say? It's a gift. I just can't believe you got out of another lunch tab."

Mor shrugged. "Hey, you have your gifts, I have mine."

The two men started back on foot after finishing their meals. Alex said, "I've got to tell you, that was the best club sandwich I've ever had." Mor had ordered Alex's usual club for him, though Sally Anne had called it a steak when she'd delivered it, a curious frown on her face.

Mor patted his stomach as he said, "Yeah, my country-fried chicken was pretty good, too. It was sweet of Irene to treat us." The handyman took a few more steps, then said, "Tonight's going to be tough on you, isn't it?"

Alex kept his gaze on the sidewalk as he spoke. "I guess I got it from Jase, but I never did care for funerals. For the longest time I swore I wasn't going to have one myself, but I'm beginning to think Jase might have had the right idea. Inviting all your family and friends to one last blowout has a touch of style that fit the man just right. I'm sorry he's gone, especially the way it happened, but I'm also happy that Jase made it back to Elkton Falls. It was wonderful getting reacquainted with him again."

Mor started walking faster as they neared his truck. Alex asked, "What's the rush?"

Mor pointed to one of the boxes they'd so carefully sealed. The top had been torn off, and a few books spilled out onto the bed. "Alex, somebody's been messing with Jase's stuff."

11

The closer they got to the truck, the more apparent it was that someone had been tampering with the boxes they'd so carefully packed. Alex and Mor jumped up into the bed of the truck and tried to see if anything was missing.

After they'd examined every box and Alex had started resealing the tops, Mor said, "I don't see that anything's gone. Alex, it was probably just some kids who couldn't resist seeing what was inside."

Alex sealed another box, then said reluctantly, "You're probably right."

Mor said, "You think it's something more ominous than that, don't you? Alex, not everything's a mystery waiting to be solved."

"Of course not," Alex said as he finished taping up the last of the disturbed boxes.

Mor looked at his friend, then said, "You don't believe that for a second, do you?"

Alex leaned against the back of the cab of the truck and

said, "Mor, somebody tried to break into Jase's cottage while I was there, and now somebody's going through his things out here in broad daylight. That either took a lot of guts, or somebody's getting desperate. Even you have to give me that."

Mor rubbed his chin. "I've got to admit, your hunches have paid off in the past. What in the world could they be looking for though?"

"I wish I knew. I'm telling you one thing; the first chance I get, I'm going to dig into this, and I won't stop until I find out what's going on."

Mor nodded. "I wish I could help, but I've got a full afternoon scheduled. Les and his lady friend are going for a picnic at Linville Falls, if you can believe that, and he's making me pay for taking the morning off." He added with a grin, "With Emma gone, I don't mind keeping busy. I've got to admit, I miss her more than I expected to, Alex."

Alex grinned at his friend. "Have you considered the possibility that was the whole point of the trip?"

Mor smiled broadly. "You could be right." He patted one of the boxes, then said, "Let's get this stuff back to the inn so I can get to work."

Steven was on the porch as Alex and Mor drove up to Hatteras West. When they got out of the truck, he joined them.

"Something I can do for you?" Alex asked.

"To be honest with you, I'm used to a faster pace than this back home. I've been to the top of the lighthouse, and I went climbing on Bear Rocks. Do you have any other suggestions for me?"

"I've got a rack full of brochures on some of our area attractions," Alex said. "I'm afraid whitewater rafting is a little much for a day trip, but there are some great places to hike around here." Alex turned to Mor. "Give me a second, will you?"

"I'll go ahead and start unloading," Mor said as he picked up one of the heavier boxes.

Steven said, "You don't have to get the brochures now, Alex, I'm not in any hurry. Do you two need a hand?"

"We've got it under control," Alex said.

"Honestly, I'm glad to help," Steven said.

Mor jumped in. "Alex, can't you see the man's desperate for something to do? Why are you depriving him? I thought you took better care of your guests than that."

Alex grinned. "Okay, you asked for it. We'd love a hand. Pick a box."

As they carried the boxes back to Alex's tiny room, Steven said, "These boxes surely are heavier than they look."

Mor was about to say something when Alex said, "Just some odds and ends I've been meaning to bring back to the inn."

After the boxes were stacked neatly along one wall of the room, Mor said, "Well, if you don't need me anymore, I'm going to hit the road."

Alex said, "Hang on a second; I'll walk you out." He turned to Steven. "Thanks again for your help. I'll be right back."

As all three men left Alex's room, he carefully locked the door behind them.

Alex stopped Mor on the porch. "Listen, thanks for everything. I really appreciate your help."

"What are friends for? Alex, you think he's a suspect, don't you?" Mor nodded toward Steven, who was lingering by the front desk.

"You bet he is. Everyone in that family is on my list."

Mor said softly, "And they're staying at the inn with you. It might not be a bad idea to watch your back. You want me to hang around? There's nothing on my list that can't wait until tomorrow."

"Thanks, but I don't need my own bodyguard yet. Besides, I know how much work you've got to do. You're coming to the send-off tonight, aren't you?"

Mor slapped Alex on the shoulder. "I wouldn't miss it for the world. You know how much I love that overgrown night-light of yours. I'm not about to miss a chance to see it fired up."

Alex nodded. "Tell you what. When you decide to tie the knot, we'll light it on your wedding day."

Mor said, "Don't hold your breath, I'm not in any hurry to walk down an aisle."

"You're closer to it than I am," Alex said with a laugh.

Mor said, "I'd say at the moment it's more of a dead heat."

After Mor was gone, Alex turned back to the lobby. It was time to talk to Steven a little more thoroughly and find out just what he might know about Jase's death.

Alex handed Steven a sheaf of brochures, then said, "I meant it when I said that your family is invited to the send-off tonight."

"I don't know, Alex. It's kind of awkward, us being involved with the missing will and all."

Alex said, "Jase wanted it to be an open invitation. My brother and I would consider it an honor if you came. All of you."

Steven hesitated, then reluctantly agreed. "If you're sure."

"I wouldn't have it any other way. Pardon me saying so, but do you have any idea what's going to happen to your father's estate if the will doesn't turn up?"

"I suppose it will ultimately be divided three or four ways. Mother isn't about to leave the outcome to fate. I've tried to talk her out of making a fuss, but if she has her way, Julie won't see a dime. I'm not so sure I'm entitled to any of my father's money, anyway. I hadn't seen him in so long, and to be honest with you, I never really tried to contact him after he left. I had him for eighteen years; that was enough for me."

"How do you feel about your newfound sister?"

Steven thought about it a moment, then said, "If Julie really is his daughter, she has more of a right to the money than the rest of us. We squandered our chances with Dad. From the sound of it, she never had an opportunity to get to know him. He was a good man in his own way, Alex. I think he stayed just as long as he could, and then the day after my eighteenth birthday, he took off. Some belated birthday present, huh?"

"How did Ashley take it?"

"She was already away at college, so it didn't affect her all that much. Truth be told, I'm worried about my big sister."

"Why is that?" Alex asked gently.

"She's been on medication for her mood swings in the past, and the depression really hits her, especially when she's under stress. I'm afraid all this about our father is stirring up all those buried feelings again."

Alex wanted to ask about his sister's claim that Steven was clinically depressed himself, but for the life of him he couldn't figure out how to bring it up without sounding like a fishwife. Instead, he shifted gears and tried another track. "Your mother must have been as mad as a wet cat when he left."

Steven said, "Alex, do you want to know the truth? She would never admit it, but I actually think she was relieved."

"Relieved about what?" Alex heard a woman's voice say as she came down the stairs. Cynthia Shays-Trask swept into the lobby, her gaze steadily on her son.

"We were just talking about tonight," Steven said guiltily.

"Come take a walk with me, Steven," Cynthia said as she locked her arm in her son's. Almost as an afterthought, she said, "I'm sure Alex will excuse us."

He didn't really have much choice. The woman had a way of imposing her will on those around her that was overwhelming.

Before the mother and son could get away, Alex said, "I was just telling Steven, you're all invited to the send-off for my uncle tonight. It's going to be right here at Hatteras West."

Cynthia turned to her son and said, "Steven, I'll meet you out on the porch."

There was no room for argument in her voice.

After her son was outside, Cynthia said, "Do you truly want us there, or are you just being polite? Don't worry about offending me, Alex. You can tell me the truth."

"My brother and I really would like you to come. You didn't know my uncle, but he would have wanted you there."

Cynthia stared into his eyes, and Alex could feel the pull of her attraction. The woman really did have a way of getting attention.

She touched his cheek lightly, then said, "In that case, we would be honored to attend. My family and I will be there, Alex."

And then she was gone.

Alex was more confused than ever about the case as he watched them start off down the path toward Bear Rocks. Could Cynthia have killed Jase herself? She appeared to be a woman who left nothing to chance. If there was the slightest possibility that she'd heard a whisper about Julie's existence, Alex could easily see Cynthia stepping in to protect her children's inheritance. What about Ashley or Steven? They could have their own reasons for wanting the will to disappear. What if Mathias had written one of them out? Alex had read about a case in Charlotte not all that long ago where a wealthy man had split his fortune between two sons in a most unusual way. One had been in and out of rehab for years, never overcoming his addictions, while the other had quietly worked hard and had prospered. Instead of a prodigal son reaction, the father had left his wayward son one dollar a year plus all the money he would use for rehab centers for as long as he lived, while his brother had inherited the balance. It had sounded like a reasonable solution to Alex, but the wayward son had fought the case for years on a technicality before losing. The whole thing had appealed to Alex's sense of justice as little did lately.

And then there was his own brother. Alex had been trying to avoid thinking of Tony as a suspect, but he was going to have to face the possibility soon. Grilling his only living relative didn't appeal to him, but Alex had no choice. He needed to know the truth, one way or another.

Alex was trying to catch up on some of the work he'd been avoiding when Elise found him folding sheets in the laundry room. "So there you are," she said. "I've been looking all over the inn for you."

Alex said, "I really am sorry, I know I've been an absentee innkeeper the last few days. It's just been kind of hectic, and I appreciate you stepping up."

Elise said, "No, that's not it. I told you to take your time. I know you've got a lot going on right now."

It was clear that there was something else on Elise's mind, but he didn't have a clue what it could be, and honestly, he was too tired to pursue it.

As Alex kept folding sheets, she said, "Maybe we can talk later. There are a few things we need to discuss."

"Absolutely." He hesitated, then said, "Could you let me

know when the caterers and the band get here? I'd like
them to set up out by the lighthouse. I checked the weather
forecast, and we should have a glorious night for it."

Elise sobered suddenly. "Are you handling everything all
right? I know it has to be hard on you, losing your uncle
like that. I can't even imagine the stress this party tonight is
adding to it."

Alex admitted, "I'm not sure a bon voyage party is the
greatest idea I've ever heard of, but one thing's certain, Jase
never did things halfway. This is what he wanted, so we're
going to do our best to give it to him." He felt himself tear-
ing up and fought the impulse. Alex was determined to
mourn Jase the way his uncle had wanted. It was the final
gift he could grant.

Elise stepped toward him, took the sheet he'd just folded
out of his hands, and said, "It's okay to grieve for him,
Alex. If you're not up to this celebration tonight, we can
still cancel it."

Alex shook his head as he said, "I can't bring myself to
go against Jase's last request. I'll say good-bye any way he
wanted me to."

She hesitated a moment, then hugged him fiercely. Alex
was surprised by the display, but before he could say a
word, Elise said, "I should have offered you my comfort
earlier, but I just didn't know if I had the right to do it.
Alex, when I saw Sandra do exactly the right thing by hug-
ging you, I wanted to crawl into a hole and die. Please forgive me for letting you down when you needed me."

Alex pulled away. "Hey, are you crying?"

"No," she said as she wiped away the evidence of her lie.
"Alex, I'm so sorry about Jase. I didn't know him long, but
he always had a smile for me."

He said, "Thanks; I truly do appreciate that. I'm just beginning to realize how much I'm going to miss him." Alex
squeezed her shoulder gently, then said, "Don't ever think

you let me down. You've always been here for me when it counted, Elise."

She started to say something more when Tony walked in. He started to back away immediately. "Whoa. Sorry to interrupt. I'll talk to you later, Alex."

"That's okay," Elise said. "I've got to finish cleaning room nine. Alex, we really should give the rooms names instead of numbers. Just think how much more impressive the Canawba Suite sounds than room nine." Before Alex could say a word, Elise added, "Just think about it, okay?" as she wiped away the last of her tears.

She left without even glancing at Tony.

Once she was gone, his brother said, "Sorry. I didn't mean to interrupt."

"She's an employee and a good friend, Tony, nothing more."

Tony rubbed his chin, then said seriously, "You should tell her that. I saw the look on that woman's face, Alex. She's smitten with you."

"She has a fiancé, Tony."

"Not for long, if I can read the signs, and believe me, little Brother, that's what I'm best at."

Alex said, "Was there something I could do for you?"

Tony shrugged. "Okay, we won't talk about it. Alex, I want us both to go up to the top of the lighthouse and rehearse the release of the ashes."

"I just figured we'd wing it. Honestly Tony, I've got a ton of work to do."

Tony said shortly, "Would it kill you to spend half an hour with your brother?"

Alex stacked the last sheet he'd folded onto the pile, then said, "Listen, I'm sorry; you're right. I know you lost your uncle, too. Let's go."

It was most likely the last thing the two brothers would ever do together in the world, and Alex couldn't blame Tony for wanting them to do it right.

12

They were all the way to the second window inside the lighthouse when Tony said, "I dropped the slip of paper with my lines on it for tonight. I'll be back in a second."

Alex said, "Can't you just do your best from memory?"

"Alex, this is important to me."

Alex said, "Okay, I'll go back down with you and help look for it."

Tony protested, "That's okay, I'm sure I dropped it at the door. You go on ahead, and I'll be with you in a minute."

Alex said, "Fine by me," as he moved up the steps.

At least the place was deserted for their rehearsal. Several townsfolk used the lighthouse as a StairMaster with a twist, and Alex tried to climb the steps whenever he could manage to get away himself. Unfortunately, running an inn didn't always give him enough free time to do that, though he did manage to get in his walk to the mailbox and back almost every day, a pretty long hike itself.

But there was nothing like being inside the lighthouse.

He caressed the walls as he climbed, feeling the coarse, cool texture as he ascended.

Alex got to the top and was relieved to find the observation platform itself deserted. That was a little unusual; normally, at least somebody was up there during the afternoon.

As promised, Tony joined him a few minutes later. Alex asked, "Did you have any luck finding your note?"

"I had it in my pocket all along," he admitted sheepishly.

Alex looked down at the two buildings of the inn, one the same as always and the other being reconstructed right beside it. He said, "I figure we'll pour his ashes out here. If there's any wind at all, they'll spread out over half of Canawba County."

"That's fine," Tony said. He hesitated a moment, then added, "Alex, we need to talk."

Alex asked, "About what?" as he took in the view he so cherished.

His brother said firmly, "It's about Jase's money."

"What about it? You got most of it, and the Preservation Society got the rest. It was nice of you to offer to share your part, but I can't take it. This is how Jase wanted it, and I'm respecting his wishes to the letter."

Tony snapped, "I'm not trying to break his will, I'm trying to give you a gift. Why can't you take it? Are you too proud to ask for help from your big brother?"

Alex said, "I honestly just want what Jase wanted me to have. Would I have accepted a ton of money from him? Absolutely. Am I happy with what he chose to leave me? You'd better believe it. His books were the most important part of his life. In a way, you got the short end of the stick, Tony."

"If I live to be a hundred, I'll never understand you," Tony said, exasperation thick in his voice.

"I never claimed to be all that easy to figure out," Alex admitted.

Tony looked out at the view, taking in the edges of the

Blue Ridge Mountains. After a period of silence, he said, "I miss him, too, you know that, don't you?"

"He was the last bit of family we had," Alex agreed.

Tony nodded. "And then there were two. It's just you and me, Bro, the last of the Winstons." He looked out into the distance another minute or two, then said, "Thanks for coming up here with me, but I know you've got a ton of work to do."

"Not a problem," Alex said as they went back inside the lighthouse. As the two brothers walked down the stairs, Alex wrestled with the possibility that Tony could have had anything to do with Jase's death. It was hard to believe that the man he'd just spoken to could have been capable of such a brutal act. Alex felt guilty for even considering it, but even as he chided himself for the thought, another voice whispered that their trip up the lighthouse steps could have all been for show, a way for Tony to make amends and ease his conscience about what he'd done. No matter how much it troubled his heart, Alex had to admit to himself that there was no reasonable way he could eliminate Tony as one of his suspects.

Elise met them at the bottom of the lighthouse.

Tony said, "Well, I'd love to hang around, but I'm heading into town to look up a few old friends. I'm glad we had the chance to talk, Alex."

"Me, too," he said as he brother headed for his car.

Elise waited until Tony was gone before she told Alex, "The sheriff just called."

Alex asked, "Has he made any progress on the case?"

"No, he wanted to know if you needed crowd control tonight. I said you'd call him back later. It sounds like most of Elkton Falls is coming out to the inn."

"I never even thought about all the people who loved Jase. Tell the sheriff to call Shantara Robinson and get her to round up her crew from the Golden Days Fair. She'll know what he means. No doubt Jase left a budget for cleanup, too, knowing him."

"I'll call him right away." Elise studied a sparkling new pendant watch pinned to her shirt, then said, "The caterers should be here in ten minutes, and the band will come along an hour later."

Alex gestured to the watch. "Is that new?"

"Yes," Elise said simply.

"From Peter?" Alex asked.

Elise said, "No, he brought it to me from my parents."

"Any reason in particular?" he asked.

Elise mumbled something, and Alex said, "Sorry, I didn't catch that."

"Today is my birthday," Elise admitted.

Alex said, "I'm so sorry, Elise, I didn't know." He added with a shake of his head, "You never exactly filled out a formal application when you came to work for me."

"You had your hands full at the time, if I remember it correctly."

"I usually do. Happy birthday, Elise. I just wish we could have celebrated it under better circumstances."

"Thanks, Alex."

He said, "You know what? I think I'll call Armstrong myself. Why don't you take the rest of the afternoon off, in honor of your birthday?"

"I can't do that to you, Alex; you've got your hands full here."

He said, "I won't take no for an answer, Elise. Think of it as my birthday present to you."

Elise said, "To be honest with you, there's nowhere I'd rather spend my birthday than at Hatteras West." The smile spreading across her face was genuine. It was the part of her that kept pulling him in, a joy in her words and heart that attracted him to her. Okay, the fact that she was stunning didn't hurt, but Alex had long since looked past her outer beauty to find the even lovelier woman just beneath the surface.

He'd have to make it up to her, missing her birthday like that. Maybe when things settled down some, he could take her out to dinner.

And then he remembered that all her evenings would be taken, now that Peter Asheford was in Elkton Falls to stay.

That evening, as the party started to gear up, Alex saw Irene Wilkins hovering near the edge of the crowd. He cut through the well-wishers and said, "Why don't you come join me?"

She had been crying, he could see that even with the fading light of the day. "I can't, Alex."

"Irene, you know you belong here. Jase would have wanted you around."

She shook her head. "I thought I could take it, but it's too painful. Forgive me," she said as she hurried away. Alex watched her go, sad that Jase's farewell party had hit her so hard. He'd have to find time to talk to her sometime in the next few weeks to reassure her that he was thrilled she and Jase had found a small corner of their lives to share with each other.

Later, with the festivities in full gear, Tony found Alex and said, "Okay, Bro, are we ready to get this farewell started?"

Alex looked over to find his brother standing nearby as he took in the crowds that had come to say good-bye.

"We might as well. Let me go talk to the band." A quartet from town had set up at the base of the lighthouse under blinking white lights Vernum had strung up in the trees. They looked like starlight up there, casting a gentle glow over the festivities. Alex had to admit, it was a good turnout, especially for a funeral. The buffet table was a hit, and several couples were dancing under the real stars.

Shantara Robinson, a friend from town who ran the general store, had asked Alex to dance, but he told her the same thing he'd told Sandra; he was there to say good-bye to Jase. Alex smiled grimly, wondering if he would have refused if Elise had asked him. He'd only seen her a couple of times since the party had started. Both times, she'd been standing close to Peter.

Alex approached the band, gave the bandleader the signal they'd agreed on earlier, and they stopped as soon as the song was over.

Alex said into the microphone, "May I have your attention please?"

Tony had deferred to him when it came to making the announcement, and Alex had reluctantly accepted. He wasn't a big fan of speaking in public—it normally petrified him—but he'd do the best he could in honor of Jase.

"First, I want to thank you all for coming out to remember my uncle Jase. Some of you might find all this a little unusual"—there were more than a few nods in the crowd—"but anyone who knew Jase understands. He was a law unto himself in many ways." There were even more nods now.

Alex gestured around him as he said, "This party was his idea, a way of saying good-bye. Thank you all for sharing it with us."

At that moment, Tony walked forward, carrying the urn that housed Jase's last remains, and all eyes were on him. As he joined Alex on the bandstand, Alex announced, "Per Jase's last request, we'll scatter the ashes from atop the lighthouse, and the lens will be turned on, one minute for every year of Jase's life."

Alex felt his knees tremble as he walked inside the lighthouse's base.

Tony cradled the urn in one arm and put a hand on his brother's shoulder. "Nicely put, Alex. You did a good job out there."

"Thanks," he said as the two men walked up the steps together, Tony carrying the urn and Alex manning the powerful flashlight that lit up the interior.

When they got to the top, Alex asked, "Do you want to scatter the ashes or light the lens?"

"Why don't we do them both together," Tony suggested. "For old times' sake."

Alex said, "Think how dramatic it will be when the light starts rotating and catches a glint of his ashes as we release them."

Tony agreed. "Tell you what, you turn on the torch all the time. I haven't done it since we were kids. You can release the ashes, and then I'll flip the switch."

Alex agreed and walked to the rail. He glanced back to be sure that Tony was at his post, then shouted to the folks clustered below a variation on Taps, "To the lakes, to the hills, to the sky," and started slowly emptying the urn as the lens came on above him. The wind gusted, shooting the flecks of gray into the night as the lens slowly started to rotate.

Alex walked quickly back inside and found Tony headed toward him. "Aren't you going to hang around and enjoy the view?"

Alex said, "No, I think it's a lot more dramatic on the ground, and we'll have the light on for over an hour this time. I want to enjoy it from the ground."

Tony said, "Suit yourself," as he brushed past Alex and went out on the deck.

Alex hurried down the steps, and Elise met him at the door, a handkerchief pressed in her hand. "Alex, that was beautiful." She studied his face, then asked, "It's hard saying good-bye, isn't it?"

"I just need some time to get used to Jase being gone. It's just beginning to sink in that he's not going to be around anymore."

Elise said, "Why don't we go inside, and I'll get you a glass of punch."

He declined. "No, I'll be all right. I need to be here."

"Alex, I insist. You can have something stronger if you'd like, but you shouldn't have to act as the host for your own uncle's farewell."

He said, "Who better, Elise? There are a lot of people here I need to talk to."

"Just come inside for a minute or two, Alex. You can collect yourself before you face them all again."

He found himself agreeing. Elise led him through the crowd, and as the band started up, a great many people began to dance again. As Alex walked up onto the porch, he looked up at the lighthouse and saw the beam cutting through the clear night above him. A single figure was outlined in each sweep, casting an eerie light over Tony as he looked down on them all.

Alex started to sit down in one of the rocking chairs in the lobby when he saw that the door to his room was slightly ajar. He knew he'd kept it locked since moving Jase's things in with him. Alex ran to the door as Elise followed with a cup of punch.

"What is it, Alex?"

"Somebody broke into my room," he shouted as reached the doorway.

Inside, it was a complete disaster. The boxes Alex and Mor had so carefully packed were dumped on the floor in a jumbled mess. Had the thief found what he'd been looking for? Alex had no way of knowing, but there was a gnawing feeling in the pit of his stomach that he'd missed something important, some clue to his uncle's murder. But had the killer found it, or was it still somewhere in that mess?

No doubt about it, the party had been the perfect excuse to break in while Alex was occupied outside. Whoever had done it had the nerves of a cat burglar, with most of Elkton Falls just outside.

Alex slumped against the bed, dislodging a book from the pile as it clattered to the floor.

13

Elise, following close behind, asked, "Alex, who would do this?"

"Somebody was obviously looking for something among Jase's things. I can't help wondering if they found it."

"Why do you say that?"

Alex started putting books back into their boxes. "They're not here, are they? It was a pretty thorough search, so I've got to believe they got what they came for."

As Elise knelt beside him and started helping, she said, "Not necessarily. This looks like whoever was in here got frustrated when they didn't find what they were looking for. Why else would the books be slammed around like this? You certainly would be hard-pressed to find anything in this mess right now."

That thought hadn't occurred to him. "You know, you could be right. But what could they have been after? Tony got the only valuable things there were in Jase's estate."

"I wish I knew," Elise said as she started on another pile of books.

Alex said, "Elise, you don't have to do this, especially not on your birthday. Why don't you go and enjoy the party. Peter's probably already wondering where you are."

"I sent Peter back to town an hour ago," she said without further explanation.

Alex didn't say another word about it as they worked side by side putting things right again. After the boxes were repacked, Alex studied the lock on his door. The frame was splintered where someone had forced their way in. "I'll have to fix this tomorrow," he said, "But for tonight, I'll have to stand guard."

He started to leave the room, then hesitated at the door. "If you're right and the thief didn't find what he was looking for, how am I going to secure the room in the meantime? I've got at least a hundred people out there I need to talk to."

"Tell you what. Why don't I stay while you make your rounds? I'm not in much of a partying mood right now."

Alex said, "I'm not leaving you here alone."

Mor wandered in and saw the splintered door frame immediately. "Geeze, Alex, maybe you should have tried your key first."

"It looks like somebody's still after Jase's things," Alex said.

Mor nodded. "I can fix that for tonight, but you're going to have to replace the door frame in the morning. It's not going to be pretty, but it should work just fine."

"What did you have in mind?" Elise asked.

"I can patch the splintered part with new wood, reinforce the whole thing with longer screws, and tighten it up in heartbeat. Alex, do you still keep your tools under the registration desk?"

"Yes, but I don't want you to have to work tonight."

Mor shrugged. "Nobody's dancing with me; I think they're all afraid of Emma, even if she is a couple of hundred miles away. This won't take long."

Alex nodded. "Let me grab my tools, and we can fix it together."

Mor said, "I can handle this, buddy. Go on out there. Everybody's wondering where you moseyed off to."

"Thanks," Alex said.

"All part of Mor or Les's service, Alex. You and Elise go on now. I've got this covered."

Alex and Elise walked out onto the porch and watched the crowd spinning around on the makeshift dance floor. He looked up at the lighthouse and watched as the beacon spun silently around again. It would be lit for another half hour, and there were no signs the party would break up any time soon after that. Whoever had broken into Alex's room had soiled his inheritance by pawing through it, but Alex wasn't going to let the burglary spoil Jase's farewell. The lighthouse, shining in all its glory, seemed to cleanse the anger from his heart. This wasn't the time to track down thieves and killers.

This was Alex's last chance to say good-bye to a man who had meant the world to him.

Alex considered asking Elise to dance as the music started up again, then changed his mind when he thought about how hard it would be for him to hold her in his arms, especially if it was for just one dance. Most likely it wouldn't mean anything special to her, regardless of what Tony had said, but he couldn't say the same thing about his own heart.

Shantara was by the punch bowl, so Alex excused himself from Elise's presence and walked over to her. "Can I cash that rain check for a dance?"

Shantara smiled, "I'd be delighted."

As the two of them danced, Alex asked, "You aren't even going to give me a hard time about saying no before?"

"I figure you've got enough on your mind," she said. "Besides, I knew you couldn't resist my charms all night."

Alex laughed, in spite of the way he felt. He and Shantara had been friends since kindergarten, and she was the closest thing to a sister that he'd ever had. She always knew how to make him laugh.

After the song was over, Sandra came over and joined them. "Since the self-imposed ban on dancing seems to have lifted, I believe you owe me a dance, sir."

Alex nodded. "You're absolutely right."

As Alex and Sandra started dancing to the next song, Shantara caught his attention and gestured to the porch. Elise was there, watching every move. Maybe he'd ask her to dance after this one was finished, despite the rumblings in his heart.

Sandra asked, "How are you holding up?"

"I'll be okay. It's tough going, though."

Sandra rubbed his shoulder gently. "If you need me, my offer still stands. You know you can call me anytime."

"Thanks. I might just take you up on that."

Though the music kept playing, Sandra suddenly stopped dancing and said, "I can't believe it."

"What's wrong?" Alex asked. "I didn't step on your foot, did I?"

Sandra gestured toward one edge of the crowd. "Julie and Amy are here. I told her to stay away from Hatteras West until we cleared this mess up."

"You can blame me, Sandra. I invited them myself," Alex said.

"You shouldn't have done that, Alex, and they never should have accepted. I'm going to take care of this right now."

Alex followed closely behind. Before he could welcome them, Sandra said, "Julie, I told you yesterday, this isn't a good idea."

Julie said, "Sandra, I'm not going to bury my head in the

sand because of the way other people act. I have every right
to be here, certainly as much as they do." Though she was
speaking to her attorney, her glare was locked on the Trask
clan, hovering near the punchbowl and as yet unaware of
her presence.

Sandra said, "I still don't think—"

Alex interrupted, "That you should be standing here
while there's music playing. Julie, may I have this dance?"

She agreed with a grim smile as she followed Alex out
onto the makeshift dance floor. The only problem was that
the second he took her in his arms, the music stopped.

"That was the shortest dance in recorded history," she
said with a smile.

Alex said, "That wasn't the real thing; it was just the
warm-up."

Then Harley Stouffers, the man who owned Quality
Garage and doubled as the quartet's keyboardist, announced, "We're taking a short break now, folks, but we'll
be back in ten minutes for more of your listening pleasure."

Alex smiled. "I just can't win."

Julie laughed, then said, "Tell you what. Let's stand right
here, and when the band starts up again, we'll be ready."
She looked up at the lighthouse and said, "It's quite lovely,
isn't it?"

"I wasn't sure you were going to be able to make it,"
Alex said.

"Between Amy and Sandra, I didn't think I was coming
myself, but the second I saw that beam, I knew I had to
come. I'm suprised you don't light it every night, Alex."

He grinned. "I would if I could, but I have to pay a fine
every time I fire it up unless the town council approves it
ahead of time."

"So you're breaking the rules in your uncle's memory?
That's so gallant."

Alex admitted, "Don't give me too much credit, Julie.
Jase got the town council to approve this before he died. I

couldn't believe he got them to grant over an hour of opera-
tion in writing."

Julie watched the beam spin around again before saying,
"Jase was a special man, wasn't he? How many of us have
the foresight to plan our good-byes thoroughly and so
well?"

"It's a real loss to everyone in Elkton Falls," Alex said,
glad that someone had actually said something to him about
Jase. Certainly the party was being thrown in his honor, but
a part of Alex wished that others would be a little more
forthright in recalling why they were gathered at Hatteras
West. Alex supposed it was Jase's own fault; he hadn't
wanted a testimonial, but a party, instead.

Well, he was certainly getting what he wished for. It was
just too bad Jase wasn't around to enjoy it himself.

Soon the music started up again, and Julie glided into
Alex's arms. As they danced, he saw that Elise wasn't on
the porch anymore. Instead, she was dancing with Mor, so
the door must have been repaired to the handyman's satisfaction. No doubt it was stronger, if not prettier, than it had
been before. Alex wondered what Emma Sturbridge would
think of Mor and Elise dancing, smiling at the thought.

When the song was over, Julie stepped out of Alex's
arms. "Thank you for the dance, kind sir."

"Thank you," Alex said. He saw a cloud cross Julie's
face. "What's wrong?"

"I can't believe she's actually coming over here."

Alex turned to find Cynthia Shays-Trask storming toward them. He had to give Julie credit; she wasn't backing
down.

Before Cynthia could get to them through the crowd of
people, Sandra joined them and took Julie's arm. "I'm getting you out of here right now, and I'm not taking no for an
answer."

"I'm not afraid to face her down," Julie said.

Amy approached. "Julie, this isn't the time or the place

for a confrontation. Out of respect," she added as she gestured toward Alex.

Julie nodded, "I didn't consider that. Alex, I'm sorry. Everyone else was right; I shouldn't have come."

He said, "Nonsense. Then we never would have had our dance. Thanks for your presence and your condolences. I greatly appreciate the gesture."

"You're very welcome, Alex."

As Julie turned away, Cynthia called out, "Young lady, I need to have a word with you."

Sandra told Amy, "Take her back to your house. I'll be over a little later."

As they disappeared into the crowd, Cynthia came on with fire in her eyes.

Sandra stepped in front of her in a neat blocking maneuver and said, "She has nothing to say to you."

Cynthia snapped, "Out of my way. She doesn't have to say a word, but she's going to hear me out. I won't stand for this."

Sandra said coolly, "I'm afraid you don't have any choice."

Cynthia snapped, "You just try to stop me."

"I'd be delighted." Alex recognized the tone in Sandra's voice and didn't envy Cynthia. The iron there was unmistakable.

"Don't think I'm going to just roll over and play dead for you people," Cynthia said when she realized that Julie was gone.

"I would be disappointed in you if you did," Sandra said.

Cynthia clearly didn't know how to react to that. She turned and headed back to the inn, and only then did Alex see Ashley and Steven on the porch, waiting in the shadows for their mother.

Cynthia had lost the battle, but it was clear to all who'd just witnessed the confrontation that the war was still far from over.

• • •

After the guests were finally gone, Shantara's famous teenage cleaning crew swept through the grounds like human vacuums, picking up every piece of litter in sight. In order to see well enough to collect the trash, they had parked their cars and trucks with the headlights pointing inward, lighting up the land around the lighthouse like broad daylight.

Sandra handled the payment; as Alex had suspected, Jase had provided for it in his will. The attorney was the last one to leave. As she was getting into her BMW, she said, "I'm going to miss him, Alex. It was one fine send-off."

"He would have approved, wouldn't he?"

Sandra said, "Oh, yes. He told me once that his only regret setting this up was that he wouldn't be around to see it." Sandra looked up at the extinguished light above them, always a very real presence on the grounds. "He truly loved your lighthouse, Alex."

Alex stared up at the structure. "So why didn't he ask to see it lit when he could enjoy it? All this doesn't make sense. We should have had this party while he could still be a part of it."

Sandra touched his shoulder lightly. "You're right, but in a very real way, he was here tonight. It was exactly the good-bye he wanted. Good night, Alex."

Alex said, "Good night, Sandra. Thanks again for handling everything."

She shook her head. "Don't thank me. Jase did all the work. All I had to do was follow his instructions."

After she was gone, Alex was finally alone. He wanted to forget, just for a few moments, how his uncle had died and focus instead on how the man had lived. He was just settling back into a rocker on the dark porch when he heard someone approach. "Mind if I join you?"

He was so startled he nearly fell off his chair. It was Vernum, and for the first time Alex could remember, the man had engaged him in conversation, instead of the other way around.

"Pull up a chair," Alex said.

Vernum settled instead on the bottom step, resting his back against the rail. "I just wanted to say that your uncle was a fine man, Alex."

"Did you know him?" Alex asked, wondering what could have possibly brought the two men together.

"Our paths crossed a lifetime ago." Vernum started to explain when the door to the inn opened. Before Alex could turn to see who was coming out, Vernum was gone. What an odd fellow he was, but no more unusual than most of the other inhabitants in and around Elkton Falls. They seemed to be drawn to the place like magnets, not resting till they settled there.

"Hello," Alex said as the front door closed. His vision had adjusted to the darkness, and he had no trouble making out his guest.

Ashley Trask-Cooper looked startled to find Alex sitting alone in the darkness. "Alex, is that you? Why are you out here all alone?"

"To be honest with you, it's the first chance I've had today to get away by myself."

Ashley turned back to the door. "Then I'll leave you to your solitude."

Alex said, "Don't rush off. Actually, I could use the company."

Ashley leaned against the railing and stared at the darkened lighthouse. "Why did you turn it off?"

"It ran its course, one minute for every year of Jase's life," Alex explained. "That's all the time the town council would allow."

Ashley said wistfully, "Your uncle must have been a true romantic. It sounds like something Donald would do. He's my husband."

"Why isn't he with you?" Alex asked softly.

"Father specified in his will that it was to be just the three of us here this week, our original little family. I'm sure he had no idea what was going to happen." She sighed, then added, "I've been so mad at him for so long, my heart goes cold whenever I think about him."

"Surely he wasn't all bad," Alex said.

"I know he was only human, but he abandoned us, Alex, and I doubt I can ever forgive him, certainly not as quickly as Steven has."

Alex looked into the night, then said, "Siblings don't always agree, do they?"

Ashley said, "Not in my house they didn't." She brushed her hands together, as if freeing them of crumbs. "Let's change the subject," she said, "to something more pleasant." She looked around the grounds and said, "It must be quite wonderful running your own business. You don't have to answer to anyone."

Alex laughed. "Don't you believe it for one minute. As an innkeeper, I'm working for a new boss every time another guest checks in. I do everything in my power to make everyone's stay a good one, but it's not always easy. Don't get me wrong, I love what I do, but it can be a real challenge at times."

"I suppose," she said. "Still, the place has grown on me."

Alex remembered Ashley's remarks when she first came to Hatteras West. Had she truly undergone a change of heart, or was she trying to get on Alex's good side for some unknown reason?

"Well, it's been a long day," Ashley said as she moved toward the door.

"Good night," Alex called to her.

After she was gone, Alex stayed on the porch, taking in the sweet sounds of the night, wondering what tomorrow would bring.

A sharp scream came from inside, shattering the calm he was just beginning to feel.

"Help! Someone help me!"

Alex rushed inside, fearful of what he was about to find. The voice, though distorted by the scream, was one he'd just heard.

Ashley was in trouble.

14

Alex found Cynthia already in Ashley's room by the time he got up there.

"What happened?" he asked, slightly out of breath as he searched the room with a quick glance.

"Someone . . . someone was up here," Ashley said as she pointed to the open window.

The curtains fluttered in the breeze, and Cynthia said, "Now, now, Ashley, it was most likely just the wind."

Ashley said fiercely, "I'm telling you, mother, when I unlocked my door, I heard someone scrambling around inside. By the time I got the door open, they were gone." She looked fiercely at her mother. "I closed that window before I came downstairs for the wake."

Cynthia said, "Perhaps Alex or his cleaning lady opened it."

Alex shook his head. "I was tied up outside during the festivities, and Elise wouldn't go into a guest's room after five P.M. unless she was invited to do so. We don't turn down the covers at Hatteras West unless it's requested ahead of time."

Elise joined them and said, "I heard a scream. What happened?"

Alex ignored her question for the moment. "Elise, did you open this window today?"

She shook her head. "Absolutely not. I haven't been in this room since eleven this morning. Now, will someone please tell me what happened?"

Cynthia explained, "Ashley thinks someone was in her room tonight."

"Mother, why don't you believe me? What possible reason would I have to lie?"

Cynthia said, "No one's accusing you of lying, dear, but you could be mistaken."

Alex walked over to the window. He looked outside but couldn't see anyone on the roof. It was possible, though, that someone really had been there. The porch roof was just below Ashley's room, and someone determined enough could climb up and gain access. So why hadn't he heard anyone climbing up? Alex had been sitting there quietly for some time. Surely he would have heard something. Unless the trespasser had gone in through the room door, then made their escape when Ashley had suddenly reappeared. Once again, whoever had broken in had real guts; either that, or a complete disregard for being caught. A thought suddenly struck him. The boldness required to climb out Ashley's window was the same kind of fearlessness needed to break into Alex's room. But what did Ashley have that the burglar could want? Was it possible that whoever had wrecked Alex's room had just been looking for something tangible to steal, like cash or jewelry? Anther idea blossomed. Could the thief have been the prowler Steven thought he saw earlier?

Alex asked, "Ashley, do you have any valuables with you, like expensive pieces of jewelry or anything like that?"

Ashley showed Alex a sizable emerald that hung from a

chain around her neck as she said, "Just this, but I was wearing it all day. I never take it off."

"Still, the thief might not have realized that when he broke in here."

Cynthia said, "So you suspect this shadow was after my daughter's necklace? Alex, you surely don't believe you have a burglar loose in your inn, do you?"

Admitting that was the last thing Alex wanted to do, but he didn't have much choice, given the circumstances. He believed Ashley had really seen someone, even if her mother didn't. "It's a possibility worth considering, Cynthia. Ashley, do you have any idea what the necklace is worth?"

She shook her head as she toyed with the stone. "It belonged to my father's mother. I've never had it appraised, but I understand it's quite valuable. Oh, Alex, do you think that's what the intruder was after? I suddenly don't feel safe here."

Alex said, "Elise, let's move her into Room 7. Ashley, it's at the back of the inn, and there's no easy way to get up there, since the porch just comes around the front of the building." Cynthia started to say something when Alex held up his hand and continued. "Honestly, I don't think you have anything to worry about, but I imagine you'll sleep better in another room. What do you say?"

"I hate to admit it, but I think you're right. Thank you, Alex."

"My pleasure. Elise, would you mind making sure she gets moved and settled in?"

"Absolutely," Elise said as she stepped up. "I'll even help her pack."

Alex said, "Cynthia, may I speak to you a moment?"

"Whatever about?"

Alex motioned outside. "Please. It won't take long."

Cynthia nodded and joined him in the hallway. Once the door was closed, Alex said, "Why don't you see if you can convince Ashley to keep her necklace in our safe? That should ease her mind while she's here."

"Alex, in the first place, I doubt anyone could persuade her to take that emerald off her neck. She has an inordinate attachment to it. And in the second place, I honestly think it was nothing more than the wind. My daughter has a tendency to overreact, and I can't help believing this is just another instance in a long line of histrionics. She hasn't always been well, if you must know."

Steven came bounding up the stairs. "What's all the fuss about? Someone downstairs said they heard a scream. It wasn't Ashley, was it?"

Cynthia said, "She thought she saw someone outside her room. Where were you, young man?"

Steven admitted, "I was with Sandra in town. We had a cup of coffee at a place called Mama Ravolini's."

Cynthia said, "You actually consorted with that turncoat?"

"It's not like that, Mother. We didn't discuss the case at all. As a matter of fact, we were catching up on old times. We went to school together, remember?"

"Oh, I remember, all right," Cynthia said, making it sound like some kind of accusation. It was clear to Alex that she didn't approve of her son keeping company with the opposing counsel at all.

Alex said, "Did you see anything suspicious on your way in?"

"I'm sorry, everything was quiet when I came back. Listen, I want to check on Ashley, just to be sure she's okay."

He started toward her room, but Cynthia said, "Steven, there's really no need to get worked up over this. She's making a great fuss over nothing."

Steven said, "I'll feel better once I'm sure she's all right myself."

After he was gone, Cynthia said, "Honestly, sometimes I

wonder how my children manage without me. Do you have any of your own, Alex?"

"No," he answered.

"Sometimes I envy single people that." Cynthia added, "Don't misunderstand me, I love my children, but they can be so difficult at times."

Tony came up the stairs and said, "Hey Alex, got a second?"

"We're in the middle of something right now," Alex said.

Cynthia said, "Go on, Alex, I can handle this situation well enough. Goodness knows I've done it enough in the past."

"I'd really rather stay," Alex said firmly.

"You heard the lady; she can handle it." Tony paused, then said, "Handle what?"

Alex said, "One of my guests spotted an intruder in her room."

Cynthia said, "Alex, I'm certain my daughter was mistaken."

Tony tugged at his sleeve. "Come on, Alex, this can't wait."

Alex reluctantly followed Tony downstairs after telling Cynthia he'd be right back. "What's so urgent?"

"There's been a change in plans. I'm leaving Hatteras West tonight. Let's face it, Alex, chances are I won't be back. I just thought you'd want to say good-bye one last time."

Tony couldn't leave, not while he was still a suspect. Alex didn't even want to think about what it would mean to him on a more personal level. Though the two of them had never been close, if Tony left now, while Alex still hadn't resolved his suspicions, the chasm would stay between them forever.

"You can't go now," Alex said.

"Why not? We held the send-off, and Sandra read the will; no offense, but there's nothing left in Elkton Falls for me. We didn't get along as kids, and I don't see that changing now."

"Are you ready to give up the last chance we've probably got to make peace between us?" Alex asked softly. It was his trump card, the last thing he could say to keep Tony there.

Tony looked at his brother carefully, then said, "You really want me to stay?"

"I do," Alex said sincerely.

"Okay, then, but I'm still leaving tomorrow night. No matter what. Alex, you're a hard man to figure."

Alex said, "Thanks for staying."

Tony headed back upstairs to his room. "I was going to grab my bag and go after we talked. I guess I'll go unpack."

After Tony was gone, Alex felt a tremor of relief. At least he'd bought another twenty-four hours to find out if his brother was a murderer and hopefully clear the air between them if he wasn't.

It wasn't much time, but it would have to do.

First thing in the morning, Alex was going to have to push in several different directions and see which one pushed back.

Elise was already sweeping the lobby floor when Alex walked in the next morning.

"You're getting an early start on things," he said.

She said, "Alex, I need a favor."

"You've got it," Alex answered.

Elise stopped sweeping and studied him for a moment. "Don't you even want to know what it is?"

"Elise, you wouldn't ask if it wasn't important to you. Just tell me how I can help."

She said, "I need to take off around ten this morning, and I won't be back until sometime after five. I can still do the rooms before I go, at least the ones that are clear of guests."

Alex asked, "Would it help to go now? I can take care of the rooms by myself today. Goodness knows you've covered enough for me lately."

Elise said, "Why are you being so nice?"

Alex answered, "You've been running this place the last few days without any help from me. I figure you're entitled to some time off. Do you want to borrow the truck?" Elise often did that when she wanted to run errands around Elkton Falls and beyond, since she didn't have transportation of her own.

"No, Peter's coming by to pick me up. Are you sure you don't mind?"

Alex wasn't thrilled by the prospect of her disappearing with Peter, but she was a grown woman, engaged to the man, for goodness sake. She could do whatever she wanted. "Take all the time you need."

She put the broom away and said, "Then I'll call him now." As she passed Alex, she said, "Thanks, I really do appreciate this."

Alex nodded, and less than ten minutes later, Peter was at the door. It was a trend he wasn't going to be all that thrilled about, the fact that Asheford was now only a quick phone call away.

Alex said, "Elise asked me to tell you she'll be down in a minute or two."

He tried to go back to his list, figuring out what order to attack it in since he was working solo today. The main thing, in all actuality, was avoiding conversation with Peter.

It wasn't going to happen though, with the man hovering nearby.

Peter coughed once, and when Alex looked up, Elise's fiancé said, "Interesting place you've got here, Alex."

"You mean the lighthouse and the keepers' quarters? Thanks, I think Hatteras West is kind of special myself."

Peter smiled. "No, I didn't mean that in particular, though it is rather magnificent. I was referring to all of Elk-

ton Falls. How did the name come about, do you know?
There must have been a great many elk here at one time, I
imagine."

Every school kid in town had cut their teeth on the story.
Alex said, "In all of this area's recorded history, there has
never been a single elk spotted within twenty miles of the
place."

Peter raised one eyebrow. "And I suppose there are no
waterfalls nearby, either."

"Not a one," Alex said truthfully.

"Then how do you explain the name?" Peter said, a
shortness in his tone that showed his frustration with being
wrong.

"The man in charge of updating and recording the names
for cities in North Carolina back in the 1800s was not very
happy about his stay here on his way through town. Evidently the man woke up in a bad mood the day he rode in,
and it proceeded to get worse as his time here wore on.
When he found the tavern was completely full, he was
forced to sleep outside in the cold rain. The next morning,
he ran into a grizzled old man who offered him the worst
breakfast he'd ever had in his life, a cold porridge that
could glue boards together. The government man asked the
codger what the name of the town was, and the old fellow
replied it was Elkton, which happened to be the old man's
name and not the name the city fathers had chosen at all.
The young man looked around the town in disgust and said,
'Well, all I can say is I hope that someday soon, Elkton
Falls!' With that he rode off, and in a fit of anger, he
recorded Elkton Falls in his book, hoping that his predic-
tion would come true someday. It's the honest truth that
there's never been an elk spotted in town, and the closest
waterfall, if you can call it that, is all the way over in Gran-
ite."

Peter wasn't buying any of it, but the story was true, as
far as Alex or anyone else in town knew.

Elise came over as Alex finished his story, but Peter wasn't ready to let it go. "So what was the town's original name?"

"Canawba Valley. To be honest with you, I like Elkton Falls a lot better, myself."

Elise said to Peter, "You asked him about the origin of the town's name, didn't you?"

"Don't tell me you actually believe his story, Elise."

She said, "I've heard it a dozen times around town; he's not making it up."

Peter shook his head as they walked out the door. "Utterly amazing," he said a few times before they made it out.

And then he was gone, with Elise by his side.

Alex had been happy enough to let Elise go before he'd discovered Peter was involved, but there was another, ulterior motive that made him even happier he'd sent her off early.

Cleaning the guest rooms by himself would give Alex the opportunity to search for whatever clues he could find that might point to Jase's killer. In Alex's opinion, every suspect involved with the case, with the exception of Julie Hart, was staying at Hatteras West, at least until that night. As he finished straightening up the lobby, Alex realized that Julie had access to the inn herself, being so close to Hatteras West. Certainly, it was a long drive from Amy's to the inn, but if Julie cut through the woods, she only had two miles to cover, and the young woman certainly looked fit enough to make that round trip easily.

But Alex couldn't worry about her now. At the moment, he had to focus on the guests staying with him at Hatteras West. If nothing came of his in-house investigation, then he could turn to Julie as a suspect. Besides, the sheriff was probably covering that ground himself.

It was time for Alex to look where no one else was searching.

•   •   •

Tony was the first one up. He met Alex in the lobby. "Hey Alex, do you have any interest in going to Hiddenite with me today? Since I've got the time, I thought it might be a fun trip."

The two had gone there countless times searching for gems as boys. It had been one of the few times Tony and Alex had actually gotten along.

"I wish I could, but Elise is off for most of the day, and I've got to hang around here and run things."

Tony said, "That's fine, I'll stay with you, then."

The last thing Alex wanted was Tony hanging around the inn, especially when he wanted to search his brother's room.

Alex said, "Tell you what. Why don't you go on to Hiddenite, then pick something up at Buck's for lunch for us on your way back, and we'll eat out on the porch. I should have a lot more time this afternoon."

Tony said, "I suppose I could do that. See, Alex, this is why I've been telling you to sell this white elephant. You're as tied to this place as if you were married to it."

"I love being an innkeeper, Tony. What else would I do with myself if I weren't running Hatteras West? Listen, have a good time. I'll see you around lunchtime."

Tony agreed, and after Alex was certain the BMW was long gone, he headed up to his brother's room.

It was time to do a little spying.

Tony had made his own bed, and his suitcase was at the foot of it, packed and ready to go. There was a lock on it, and ordinarily, Alex wouldn't dream of prying it open. However, the issue of personal privacy didn't concern him all that much at the moment, not when he was looking for a possible clue about Jase's murder. Alex tried to convince himself that he was looking for proof Tony didn't do it as much as evidence that he might have. In his heart, no matter their past differences, Alex didn't want his brother to be guilty, but logically, he couldn't dismiss him, either.

Fortunately, he didn't have to do anything as drastic as breaking into the luggage. Alex locked the door and headed down to the main desk. In a drawer there, he had a ring filled with master keys to just about every suitcase brand made, all except the custom lock jobs. Too many of his guests had locked themselves out of their own luggage over the years, and Alex had bought the keys from a friend in NewCon who ran a locksmith service.

Alex was just opening the drawer when Ashley came downstairs.

"What are doing, Alex?"

"Just looking for a lost key," he said.

Ashley asked gently, "Do you have a minute?"

He nodded. Tony should be gone for a while. "What's on your mind?"

"I want to apologize for last night. Mother's probably right; I do have an overactive imagination at times. Nothing seems to have been taken. I must've been mistaken. Sorry for all the trouble."

"No trouble at all," Alex said. He wasn't so sure she was right. With all that was going on at the inn, it was too easy to believe that someone had indeed crept into Ashley's room without her knowledge. He didn't have the slightest desire to tell her that, though.

Alex said, "So, where are you off to today?"

"I thought I'd check out Bear Rocks. Steven told me they were really quite fascinating."

Alex nodded. "Enjoy yourself, but be careful. Some of those rocks are tough to climb if you're not used to them."

Alex slid the master key ring back into the drawer. Tony's room would have to wait, since he'd be gone most of the morning, tied up in Hiddenite.

Alex was going to search Ashley's room while he had the chance and see if anything turned up there.

15

Ashley Trask-Cooper wasn't nearly as neat as Alex would have expected. Clothes were thrown everywhere, as if she'd worked for hours putting together the perfect outfit from everything she'd brought with her for her week's stay at Hatteras West. He neatly folded all her clothes and put them in the bureau drawers, all the time searching for some sign of evidence that Ashley had been involved with Jase's murder or the burglary of his room the night before.

After putting her clothes away, changing the sheets, and cleaning the bathroom, the room was neat, but there was no evidence that Ashley had been the one who'd gone through Jase's things.

He was nearly finished with the room when he noticed a book on the edge of Ashley's nightstand. For a moment he thought it was the title he'd taken from Jase's cottage, but when he looked closer, he saw that it was *Treasure of the West*, not *The Treasure Below* title he'd picked up there, or *The Treasure in the Hills* from Jase's office. What was remarkable was that the three books came from the same series! What were the odds of that? Could this one have come from Jase's library? Alex couldn't remember if he'd handled the book himself; the titles had blurred after a while. It might even have been one that Mor packed.

Alex picked up the book and leafed through it, but there was no indication that it had ever belonged to Jase. His uncle didn't go in for bookplates or inscriptions.

Alex was just setting it back down when a key turned the lock and the door opened.

Ashley said abruptly, "Alex, what are you doing in my room?"

Alex said smoothly, "Elise has the morning off, so I'm cleaning the rooms myself today. I was dusting the nightstand, and I accidentally knocked your book off. I'm afraid I lost your place."

Ashley took the book from his hands as she said, "Oh, it's some dreary thing I picked up at a dusty little bookshop in town to help me sleep. I've got to read something, or I can't nod off at night." She looked around the room. "I'm sorry it was such a mess before. I meant to clean it up myself before you got to it."

Alex smiled. "Compared to a lot of my guests, you're a neat freak. You weren't able to spend much time at Bear Rocks, were you?"

"I decided to climb the steps of the lighthouse instead, so I came back for my running shoes. Care to join me?"

Alex said, "I wish I could, but I've got a lot of work still ahead of me."

"A rain check, then." She tucked the book in her travel bag, then said, "If you'll excuse me?"

"Of course. I'm finished up in here."

After Alex was out in the hallway, he headed straight for his room. Locking the door behind him, Alex looked up

Hannah Parsons's number in the phone book. She ran Hannah's Book Shoppe, the only bookstore in Elkton Falls.

Hannah, a happy octogenarian, answered on the first ring. "Why Alex Winston, how are you? I'm sorry about Jase. He was one of my best customers. Sorry I couldn't make it out there, but I saw the light from my bedroom window! My, what a glorious sight!"

"Glad you liked it. Hannah, I've got a question. Do you remember a book titled *Treasure of the West*? It's a hardback."

"Oh, yes, I remember it well. I sold it to a lovely young woman heading out your way for her stay at the inn. Are you looking to acquire a copy of your own? I'm on the Internet now, you know; I could do a search for you."

"No, thanks. I was just wondering." So Ashley really had come by a copy of it legitimately.

Hannah added, "Jase bought a few of the books in that series himself. *The Treasure Below* and *The Treasure in the Hills,* if memory serves. That man loved to surround himself with books."

So that mystery was solved. "Thanks Hannah, sorry to bother you."

"No bother at all, Alex. Come see me next time you're in town. I've got another lighthouse history book I'm holding for you, and there's a new bed-and-breakfast mystery series I've found that's quite nice." Alex kept a great variety of lighthouse-themed books in his inn library, along with mystery series set in small inns. It seemed his guests loved those books almost equally.

"Okay, I'll swing by next time I'm in town. Thanks again, Hannah."

"You're welcome, dear."

So that was a dead end. For the moment, Ashley was in the clear.

For the moment.

•   •   •

Steven was ringing the small bell at the front desk as Alex started out of his own room. "Can I help you?" Alex asked.

Steven said, "Hi, Alex. Mother and I are going into town, and I was wondering if you could have your maid clean our rooms while we're gone."

"I'll see to it," Alex said.

"Good enough. I've got to run; she's already waiting for me in the car."

After they were gone, Alex grabbed his ring of keys and did a quick sweep and cleanup of Steven's room first. As Alex unlocked the door, he had to fight the urge not to sneak inside. He had every right to be there, had even been invited by Steven himself. That didn't stop him from feeling guilty as he scanned the room while he cleaned, searching for any sign that Steven was not what he seemed. In the bathroom, Alex found a medication he wasn't familiar with. There were a few pills in the bottom of the small brown prescription bottle with Steven Trask's name on it. After a quick check with Doc Drake's wife and nurse, Madge, Alex discovered it was indeed meant for the treatment of depression. There had been no similar bottle in Ashley's room. So, was that proof that Ashley had been telling the truth, or that Steven had? If Ashley was undergoing treatment for depression, she was skipping her doses at Hatteras West. And if Steven had his medication with him, wouldn't that imply that he was level and steady? In the end, Alex wasn't sure what the presence or absence of medications meant.

The only other thing Alex found in the room was an open book about famous forgeries in history. Alex studied the legal pad beside it for a few minutes, then decided the notes were simply different methods of attacking Julie Hart's claim on Mathias's fortune by trying to disprove the letter that served as the only proof that Mathias had believed Julie was his own. Perhaps Steven wasn't as welcoming as he wanted the world to believe.

In Cynthia's room, Alex found another mess. As an
apple, Ashley hadn't fallen far from her mother's tree. As
Alex cleaned, he found one of the Hatteras West Inn's
notepads, stocked in every room, now filled with scribbles,
telephone numbers, and exclamation points peppered
throughout. No doubt it represented her search for legal
representation outside the confines of Elkton Falls. Alex
also found a curious item that had rolled under the bed. It
was a complete envelope with Jase's return address across
the back flap. Alex grabbed the paper and turned it over.
Cynthia's name and address were typed there, but the envelope itself was empty. The postmark was blurred, and Alex
couldn't make out a date other than the current year. So
what could it mean? Was it from the letter that had brought
the Trasks to Hatteras West, or was it a different, perhaps
newer communication from Jase? Alex started to put it
back where he'd found it, but he had the right, even the
obligation to take it in his role as housekeeper. After all,
anyone else would have considered it nothing more than
trash.

He tucked the envelope into his shirt pocket, then rapidly
finished cleaning the room.

Alex had found a number of things in the rooms of the
Trask family, but he'd be whipped if he knew what they
meant. Analyzing his finds would have to wait for another,
less frantic time.

For the moment, Alex had one more place to snoop.

Alex retrieved the suitcase key collection from the front
desk and headed back to Tony's room. It took Alex just two
minutes to find the proper key to Tony's suitcase; he'd become rather adept at it over the years, and it didn't hurt that
most luggage keys were well-marked. As the lock clicked
open, Alex decided to hurry his examination of the contents
of his brother's bag. Ashley's early entrance had startled

him, and he couldn't just explain away breaking into his own brother's bag.

Alex didn't need much time to find something in his brother's room after all. Hidden among Tony's clothes was Jase's personal journal, a book that by all rights belonged to Alex, given the contents of the will. But what should he do about it? He certainly didn't have time to read it all, and if he took it, Tony would know Alex had been in his bag. Alex scanned the last few entries, but Jase's handwriting was worse than a doctor's. It would take time to decipher the scrawls.

Alex tucked the book under his arm, then headed back downstairs. He'd make a copy of the last few weeks' worth of entries, then return the book to Tony's bag. That way his brother would never know he'd been in there.

Alex was just copying the last page when a familiar voice behind him said, "What's up, Brother?"

Tony was back!

Alex turned to Tony, making sure the copies were out of his line of sight. "Catching up on my records. You wouldn't believe the forms I have to fill out around here. You're back early. What happened to Hiddenite?"

"I decided it wouldn't be any fun by myself. Tell you what, why don't I help you finish up the rooms, then we can go to Buck's together and grab something to eat."

Alex said, "You don't want to spend your last day here cleaning, do you?"

Tony said, "Just let me change, and I'll be right with you."

Ashley came downstairs, and Alex called her over. "Still going up to the top of the lighthouse?"

"I am," she said. "Did you change your mind about the tour? I'd love to learn more about the history of this charming place." Ashley had certainly done an about-face regarding Hatteras West.

Alex said, "I'm really jammed, but my brother Tony knows almost as much about Hatteras West as I do. He grew up here, too. I'm sure he could tell you some fascinating stories about our history."

Ashley was a pretty woman, away from her husband and children, and just as Alex had guessed, Tony rose to the bait. "I know more than you've forgotten, little Brother. I'll be glad to take you, Ashley."

"Are you sure it's not too much trouble?"

Tony said, "Part of the Winston service, ma'am."

Alex whispered, "Thanks, this will really help me out."

"No problem." Tony turned to Ashley. "Are you ready for the grand lighthouse tour?"

"Absolutely."

As soon as he was sure they were well on their way, Alex folded the copies and tucked them into his back pocket. His hands didn't stop shaking until the journal was safely back in Tony's bag upstairs in his room. Alex did a perfunctory sweep of the place, straightening a few things as he searched, but he didn't come across anything else that looked out of the ordinary.

Alex decided to lock himself in his own room downstairs and see if he could come up with a way of breaking the code of Jase's handwriting, but after ten frustrating minutes, he decided he was going to have to call in an expert. After making sure Nadine was still in the office wrapping things up, Alex put a sign on the desk that said, Gone into Town. Back Soon, and left.

Tony was shouting something from the top of the lighthouse as he drove by, but Alex pretended not to hear.

"Oh, Alex, I'm thrilled you found Jase's journal."

Alex handed Nadine the photocopied pages, and she asked, "Don't you have the original?"

Alex said, "It's still at the inn." He didn't bother explaining. He wasn't ready to share his suspicions with anyone yet about exactly what Jase may have written in his journal.

"Very well." Nadine retrieved a pair of reading glasses and tackled the sheets. After a few moments, she said, "Oh, my. Are you certain you want to hear this, Alex?"

"I'm a grown man, Nadine, I can take whatever Jase had to say. Give it to me straight from what he wrote."

Nadine said, "Very well," then she started to read. " 'Alex seems happy enough fighting to keep his inn alive. It's hopeless going it alone, but his heart's in the right place. That boy needs a good woman by his side. Elise Danton? No, she's already got someone. I must see if there's anyone in town I can interest him in. That boy deserves some happiness in his life.' Alex, there's more, but it's along the same lines. Shall I continue?"

"No, you can skip ahead." He'd thought he recognized his name a few places in the pages, but that was all he'd been able to decipher. He'd deal with Jase's feelings later; right now, he was looking for clues.

Nadine continued, "Tony is in desperate need of money again. I wish I could say it was a surprise, but I'd been expecting it. There was a new twist though, an ugly one at that. He came to me today demanding his inheritance! The impudence of that boy! I'm drafting a new will as soon as I get the chance! He's out! Alex can use it all to prop up that inn, if he so chooses, or he can sell everything and make himself a fresh start! I'm finished with Tony, that's the only thing I know without hesitation or reservation. I made a mistake not giving Alex half of everything before, and I mean to correct it, and soon!" Nadine looked up. "It gets kind of blurry here; he was clearly upset when he wrote this."

"When was it dated?" Alex asked.

Nadine looked at the entry, then said, "Right after Tony's last visit." She stared at the paper, refusing to meet his gaze as she added, "Less than a week ago."

Alex had so many questions ripping through his head, he wasn't sure which one to ask first. "Obviously Jase didn't get the opportunity to write a new will. Nadine, I thought you said that the last time Tony was here was over a month ago."

Nadine kept studying the papers in front of her, refusing to meet his gaze, and Alex knew she wasn't telling him everything. "What is it? What are you holding back?"

Nadine sighed, then said, "Alex, I'm afraid I haven't been exactly forthright with you. Your brother came to see Jase four days before the murder. It was late at night, and I was already halfway down the street when I realized I'd left my purse on my desk. I started back toward the office, but then I saw that your uncle wasn't alone anymore. He and Tony were arguing about money, and something told me those two men needed some time alone. Alex, I didn't mean for you to know just how persistent Tony was about demanding his 'share' of your Uncle's money. It was breaking Jase's heart."

Alex asked, "Did you tell Sheriff Armstrong about any of this?"

Nadine said, "I couldn't bring myself to do it. Now I think I've done something horribly wrong." Her voice was barely a whisper as she added, "Alex, I think your brother killed him."

"This is too important to keep to yourself."

"What are you suggesting, Alex? Do you honestly expect me to turn your brother over to the police?"

Alex said, "Nadine, do you think I want to believe he's capable of this for one minute? It's a nightmare for me, thinking that my brother could have killed Uncle Jase. But I can't turn my back on the possibility that he did it. And if Tony killed him, he deserves to be punished for it, brother or not."

Nadine looked as if she was about to cry. "Alex, you're good at solving these things. Talk to your brother and poke around some more. Don't just turn your back on him. He's the only family you have left."

"I can't shield him if he's a murderer," Alex said.

"No, but if he's not, you're going to ruin him. You know that, don't you? Alex, don't do this for your uncle. Don't even do it for Tony. Find the truth for yourself. It's the only way you'll be able to live with the outcome, no matter what it is. Keep digging," she said with a fiery burst. "I have faith in you, Alex."

"I'm glad somebody does." Alex shoved the copies toward Nadine. "Put these somewhere safe, okay? And don't mention this conversation to anyone else. I don't want Tony to know you saw him coming back here after hours."

Nadine looked taken aback. "Alex, you honestly don't think I'm in danger from your brother, do you? My goodness, I was his teacher, too!"

"Just don't take any chances, Nadine. I'll call you later if I find anything else."

She took his hand in hers and squeezed. "Alex, you'll do the right thing. I know it in my heart."

"I just wish I knew what the right thing was," Alex answered.

"When you find it, you'll know it. Good luck."

He frowned, then answered, "I'll need it. Lock your door after I'm gone, Nadine."

"Oh, Alex, you worry too much."

Still, he waited outside the office door until he heard the meaty click of the door locking behind him before he left.

16

As Alex headed back to Hatteras West, he kept considering the possibility that his brother had killed their uncle. Could his greed have driven him to it? Sandra couldn't have known anything about Jase's intention to draft a new will; she would have said something to him. Could Jase have drafted a new document himself? Alex wondered if there had been more than one will in Jase's safe the morning he was murdered. If his uncle told Tony about the change during a confrontation between the two men, Tony could have clubbed Jase and destroyed the new will, knowing that the previous one left him all that money. Alex's guts were roiling by the time he pulled up Point Road.

Alex had to find Tony and talk to him. The possibility that his brother was a murderer couldn't stop him.

He had to know the truth.

Alex was surprised to find Elise on the front porch, sitting on one of the rockers facing the lighthouse.

"I thought you were going to be gone all day," he said.

"Plans change," Elise answered. "You did a nice job on the rooms."

"Thanks," he said absently.

"What's wrong, Alex?" Elise said levelly.

"I'm sorry. I've just got something I have to take care of. Elise, do me a favor, would you? If I'm in any 'accidents' over the next few days, tell Armstrong to check into it, no matter what it looks like."

He started to brush past her when she leapt from the chair. "What's going on?"

"Never mind. Forget it, Elise, I shouldn't have said anything."

"But you did. Alex, I'm worried."

He said evenly, "I am, too. That's why I need to talk to Tony."

Elise wouldn't get out of his way. "Why don't we take a walk, and you can tell me about it before you do whatever's on your mind."

"I'm sorry, I have to do this now," he said.

She put her hand on his and said, "Sometimes it helps to talk it through first, Alex. What have you got to lose, five minutes of your life? It might help you sort out how you feel. It's worked before."

That was true enough. Alex had often used Elise as his sounding board in the past. Maybe he was too close to Tony and Jase to look at things rationally.

"Okay, you've convinced me."

Elise smiled. "Good. Why don't we go up to the top of the lighthouse? You always seem to think better up there."

Alex looked up and saw two figures at the top. Tony and Ashley were still up there. "How about Bear Rocks instead?"

Elise followed his gaze up, then said, "Bear Rocks it is."

As the two of them walked down the path to the rock formations, Elise said, "Talk to me, Alex."

"I think my brother might have killed Jase," he said in a

burst of words. Somehow voicing them made it all seem real.

Elise said, "I know you well enough to realize you've got some evidence to back that up. What makes you think Tony might have killed your uncle?"

After Alex explained Tony's late-night visit to Jase, the angry journal entry, Tony's strong financial motive, and the possibility of his being written out of a new will, Elise said, "You've certainly built a strong case against him. Are you saying you're discounting the disappearance of Mathias Trask's will completely? It still looks like a strong motive to me."

"Tony could have taken it to divert suspicion from his real intent, Elise." There was a sudden noise in the woods nearby.

Elise said, "What was that?"

"Probably two squirrels chasing each other over territory rights."

Elise turned back to the problem. "So what are you going to do about it?"

"What can I do? I'm going to confront Tony and find out the truth."

Elise said softly, "Alex, if he did kill Jase, why would he tell you the truth? What's it going to cost him to lie to you?"

Alex shook his head. "You don't understand. It doesn't matter what he says. I can tell when Tony's lying. I've always been able to. He's never gotten away with a lie with me in his life."

"I don't know, Alex, it sounds risky to me."

"Elise, don't you see? I can't stand not knowing! If he comes after me, so be it. One way or another, I've got to know the truth."

Elise said, "Then I'll go with you. There's safety in numbers."

Alex said, "Elise, as much as I appreciate your offer,

Tony's not going to admit anything with you around. You know as much as I do now. If anything happens to me, tell Armstrong, and don't let up on him until he's cracked the case."

She leaned forward and kissed him on the cheek.

Alex pulled away and asked, "What was that for?"

"Luck."

Alex's legs were shaking as he started for the lighthouse stairs, but his condition had nothing to do with the arduous ascent ahead of him. To his surprise, Tony and Ashley met him near the bottom of the lighthouse, their tour evidently over.

"There you are," Tony said. "We were beginning to wonder about you."

Alex said, "Ashley, did you know Steven was looking for you? He said it was important."

Ashley said, "Steven's sense of importance doesn't often match mine."

Alex hated to lie, but he had to get Tony alone. "He looked a little upset to me, to tell you the truth."

Ashley said, "I'd better go find him," then disappeared quickly inside the inn.

Tony started toward the inn, too, but Alex touched his arm lightly. "We need to talk."

Tony pulled away as he said, "So, we'll talk on the front porch."

"Why don't we sit here on the lighthouse steps," Alex insisted. "We've got a lot more privacy here."

Tony said, "Fine. What's on your mind, little Brother?"

"I just have one question for you, and I want the truth. Tony, did you kill Uncle Jase?"

Tony snapped, "Have you lost your mind? What are talking about?"

Alex said, "I know Jase was cutting you out of the will, and I also know how desperate you were for money."

Tony said, "How did you find that out?" A look of suspicion crept across his face. "Did you go through my things, Alex?"

"Why not? You went through mine. I kept trying to figure out why someone would search through Jase's possessions, first when they were on Mor's truck, and then again in my room. You were looking for the journal, weren't you?"

"Get a grip, Alex. I don't know what you're talking about." All the signs were there; his brother was lying.

Alex snapped, "Come on, Tony, I found his journal in your suitcase."

Tony said, "Okay, I admit it. I took it after we left Sandra's office that day she read the will. Alex, I expected Jase to follow up right away when he said he was writing me out of his will. Nobody was more surprised than I was when Sandra read the version that left me all that money. You'd better believe the first thing on my mind was getting my hands on that journal before Armstrong started snooping around. I knew how Jase recorded everything in his life in there. I followed you over to his house, and the second you disappeared into his bedroom, I went in to look for it myself. It wasn't that tough to spot; it was right on the stand by the door. I nearly had a heart attack when you came out of that room, but I didn't have a choice. That journal would have set me up as a murderer, and I had no desire to be the sheriff's only suspect for a murder I didn't commit."

"Do you expect me to believe you, Tony?" His brother's body language, the tone of his voice, even the way he stared at Alex screamed that he was telling the truth. But that couldn't be. There were too many facts that pointed straight at his brother.

Tony jammed a finger into Alex's chest. "I told you, I'm not lying! Do you really think I could have killed him? The last time I saw Jase, he was mad as a wet cat, but he was still very much alive. Jase was furious with me the last time we spoke, and I've got to live with that for the rest of my life. I'll never have the chance to say how sorry I am about everything." Tony looked Alex straight in the eye. "I did not kill our uncle, Alex. You know what? I'm past caring what you believe. Now get out of my way. I'm leaving Hatteras West forever, and I'd advise you not to try and stop me."

As Tony blew past him, Alex knew in his heart that his brother was indeed telling the truth!

Alex hurried after him as Tony went upstairs to retrieve his bag, anxious to catch up with his brother and try to set things right between them. After all, if Tony left Hatteras West now, he knew his brother would never come back.

Alex was surprised to hear a police siren as he raced toward Tony's room. What had happened now to bring the sheriff back to Hatteras West?

Tony had his bag in one hand as he blew past Alex toward the front door.

Alex said, "Don't go like this. We need to talk about it."

Tony said, "I'm finished talking, Alex. I wish I could say it's been nice being related to you, but I'm not going to lie to you."

Alex watched him storm out the front door, thought about it for three heartbeats, then decided to go after him before his brother was gone forever.

By the time Alex reached the porch, he found Armstrong putting handcuffs on his brother.

"What's going on, Sheriff?"

"I'm taking your brother in for questioning, Alex, and I'd appreciate it if you didn't get in the way."

"On what grounds?" Alex asked with a sinking feeling in his gut.

"We just got an anonymous tip that led to a break in the case. That's all I can say." He turned to Tony. "You okay with me grabbing your suitcase, too, or do I have to get a warrant for it?"

Tony looked steadily at Alex as he said, "Go ahead. Do whatever you have to do. Just get me out of here." Armstrong started to push him into the back of the squad car when Tony added loudly, "I can't believe you, Alex. You couldn't talk to me before you called the police?"

"I swear I didn't call them, Tony," Alex said.

"Yeah, right. Thanks a lot, Brother."

After Tony was locked up in the back of the squad car, Armstrong said, "You mind grabbing that bag at your feet for me, Alex? I need to search his room, too, but I don't want to leave him alone out here in the patrol car while I'm doing it."

"Sheriff, do you honestly think I'm going to lift one finger to help you when you're trying to railroad my brother?"

Armstrong said, "I know this is hard on you, but you have to want the truth to come out. Don't you owe that much to Jase? I'm sorry, Alex, but I have to do this. I have no choice."

Alex shrugged, then said, "But I don't have to help you. Not this time."

Armstrong said, "Then we'll play it your way." He grabbed the bag at Alex's feet. "I'll take Tony into town and lock him up in a holding cell, then I'll be back out here to search his room. Don't go in there while I'm gone, Alex. That's an official police order. I'd hate to find out somebody tampered with evidence."

Alex couldn't stand the thought of his brother being locked up, but there was nothing he could do about it. "You've got my word I won't go in there."

"Good enough," Armstrong said as he got into the cruiser. Alex glanced inside the patrol car as the sheriff

drove off. Tony was staring straight ahead, not even looking in Alex's direction as he went past.

Elise met him at the door as he walked into the inn.
"What's going on, Alex?"

"As if you didn't know," he said abruptly.

"What are you talking about? Was that the sheriff? I was
in the laundry room when I heard the siren. Alex, answer
me!"

Alex refused to reply as he hurried to his room and
bolted the door behind him. He needed some time to think.
Elise was the only one he had shared his suspicions about
Tony with. She had to have been the one who phoned in the
anonymous tip to Armstrong. Alex just couldn't imagine
why she'd broken his confidences so quickly. Was it out of
some kind of misguided loyalty to him? Had she done it out
of fear for his life? Ultimately, it didn't matter why she'd
called the police. Elise had violated the trust between them,
and that was one thing he didn't think he'd ever be able to
forgive.

There was a repeated knock on his door, and he heard
Elise say, "Alex, I don't know what's wrong. Talk to me."

When he didn't reply, she finally gave up. Alex sat there
for half an hour, wondering how things had gotten into such
a mess, and how the two of them were ever going to work
together when she had shattered his trust so completely.

Ultimately, Alex realized he couldn't hide in his room
forever. He had an inn to run.

Elise was at the front desk waiting for him when he came
out.

She said, "Alex, I want to know exactly what you think
is going on here."

He shook his head as he reached for the telephone beside
her and punched in a number he knew by heart. When Sandra answered on the first ring, Alex said, "Armstrong
picked Tony up for questioning in Jase's murder half an
hour ago."

"What?" Sandra said. "On what grounds?"

"He got an anonymous tip," Alex said as he looked intently at Elise.

After explaining the facts but assuring her that he thought Tony was innocent, Sandra said, "I'll go straight over to the jail. Don't worry, Alex, I'll look into this and get back to you."

"Thanks. It's nice to be able to count on you."

After he hung up, Elise said, "Alex, it's clear you think I betrayed your trust, but I didn't call the sheriff. I would never do that."

He said, "Then how do you explain it? Who else knew about the journal in the suitcase, Elise? I didn't tell anybody but you. Nadine knew it existed, but not where I'd found it. Besides, she's the one who talked me out of calling Armstrong in the first place, remember? I just wish you would have trusted me."

Elise pleaded, "I did, Alex! I didn't call the police. Maybe Nadine had a change of heart, because I certainly didn't call the sheriff. I thought you knew me better than that."

As she raced off toward her room, there was nothing Alex could say. Elise was right; he did know that she would never go behind his back like that. With a knot in his stomach, Alex realized that he may have just driven off the best friend and the biggest ally he had.

Alex stared after her, wondering what he could do to make things right with Elise. Maybe if he called Nadine, she'd be able to clear things up. He picked up the telephone and dialed Jase's office. There was no answer. Still, it had to have been her. Nadine was the only possibility left.

Alex stared at Elise's door, regretting his earlier behavior. He hadn't even given her a chance. The stress of losing Jase to a violent murder and the guilt he felt about accusing Tony had worn Alex to the bone, and he'd taken it out on her. If Elise said she didn't call the sheriff, Alex knew in his heart he could believe her.

He knocked lightly on her room door, then louder. "Go away," Elise said in a muffled voice.

"Elise, I'm sorry. I had no right to accuse you like that."

There was nothing but dead silence on the other side of the door.

"Hey, I'm on my knees out here apologizing. You don't want to miss this."

As he heard her doorknob start to turn, Alex quickly dropped to his knees.

Elise's eyes were red as she opened the door. "I'm listening."

"I'm sorry, Elise. I was hurt and angry and looking for someone to blame, and you just happened to be in range. I shouldn't have jumped to conclusions."

"And . . ." she said, waiting for more.

"And I should have believed you when you said you didn't call Armstrong. I'm sorry."

She reached a hand down to him and helped him up. "Just don't let it happen again, Alex. You know how I feel about my word. When I say something's true, you can believe it."

"I know, I'm the same way," Alex said. "It's no excuse, but I'm really worried about Tony."

Elise said, "I'm probably going to catch grief for saying this, but how can you be so certain he's innocent now? An hour ago you were ready to convict him of murder."

Alex said, "Elise, I can't explain it, but I looked into his eyes, and I knew he was telling the truth. He didn't kill Jase."

Elise said, "Then we'd better find out who did."

"Good enough," Alex said. "The first thing we should do is to go talk to Julie and see if she might not be as innocent as she appears to be."

17

On their way out the door, Alex heard Ashley Trask-Cooper calling out to him. "Alex, I've searched the entire inn, and I can't find my brother anywhere."

It took him a second to realize that Ashley was talking about the wild-goose chase he'd sent her on so he could have some time alone with Tony.

"That's right, I forgot all about it. He went into town with your mother. You know, I think I overreacted. Sorry if I worried you for nothing."

Ashley studied him curiously for a moment, then said, "I'll be in my room if anyone needs me."

Alex said, "I'll be away from the inn for a little while, so if you need anything—"

Elise interrupted, "We'll both be gone." She tugged Alex's shirt. "I'm going with you, remember?"

Ashley said, "You mean you're both going to leave me here all by myself?"

"Ashley, you'll be fine. Vernum is around here somewhere, and we have other guests, too. Besides, I expect your family back any minute. Now if you'll excuse us . . ."

"Oh, go on," she said abruptly as she headed up the stairs.

After they were out on the porch, Alex said, "I feel bad leaving her alone."

Elise said, "Alex Winston, if you think you're going to go off investigating this without me, you're sadly mistaken. Jase wasn't my uncle, but I liked and respected the man."

Alex smiled grimly. "Admit it. You like to dig as much as I do."

Elise said, "Somebody's got to keep you out of trouble."

As they headed for the truck, Elise said, "Why didn't you question Ashley while you had the chance? She's feeling vulnerable, at least if we can believe her. She might tell you something she wouldn't ordinarily."

"I can't see her killing Jase, can you?"

"Alex, someone did. Why not Ashley? Do you honestly think she'd be more inclined to talk with her mother around? Cynthia doesn't seem to be the type to let her children go around unsupervised, no matter how old they are."

"Maybe you're right. What possible excuse can I use to talk to her now?"

Elise grinned. "Come on, Alex, turn on that charm of yours. Julie can wait while you talk to Ashley."

Alex asked, "So what are you going to be doing while I'm interrogating a suspect?"

Elise said, "I'll be eavesdropping nearby, of course."

Alex tapped on Ashley's door. It took her a moment to answer. "Who is it?" she said without opening it even the slightest crack.

"It's Alex Winston. Do you have a minute?"

Alex heard the chain come off and the lock slide open.

"Certainly. Come in. What happened to that errand you were going to run with your maid?"

Alex said, "We decided to put it off for a little while. I didn't want you to think for a minute that I'd desert you like that." Alex felt a little uneasy being alone with a female guest in her room. He added, "I was thinking we could talk out on the porch. It's such a glorious day."

Ashley agreed, and they were soon seated on a pair of rockers overlooking the lighthouse. "So what's on your mind?" she asked as she rocked gently back and forth in the breeze.

"I just wanted to check on you and see how you're handling all of this. It must have been hard for you, discovering you have a sister the day your father's will was supposed to be read."

Ashley stopped rocking. "I don't have a sister, no matter what that letter says."

"Do you think there's a chance that Mathias would lie about something as important as that?" Alex asked softly.

"I wouldn't put it past him, even if that letter is legitimate."

Alex asked, "Do you have any reason to believe it isn't?"

Ashley said, "I don't know what it could possibly hurt by telling you that Steven doesn't believe that letter is from our father at all. If you can believe it, he's been holed up in his room studying a book about forgery techniques to prove Father never wrote it in the first place."

"But what if it is real?"

"If you're looking for motives for my father's erratic behavior, you're not going to have much luck asking me. I never did understand him."

"He sounds like he was a fascinating man," Alex said as he noticed Vernum trimming the lower branches of the trees near the inn. At least Ashley couldn't see him from her spot. Alex only hoped the arborist didn't come any closer and interfere with his questioning.

After a few moments of silence, Ashley said, "He was quite aggravating as a father. I can't imagine how much more exasperating he was as a husband. I honestly don't know how Mother put up with him for as long as she did."

Alex asked, "She divorced him right after he left, didn't she?"

Ashley shook her head. "That's a common misconception Mother wants the world to believe. Why, my own brother doesn't even know they aren't really divorced. Mother got tipsy one night and confessed to me that she'd never bothered, thinking that someday it might be to her advantage to still be married to him."

"Now that's interesting," Alex said, slowly rocking in the chair.

"What do you mean?" Ashley asked.

"Well, if there is a significant estate, and everyone seems to think there is, she most likely stands to get a healthy cut of it."

"And she deserves every penny she gets, Alex!"

"I'm not saying otherwise," Alex quickly added.

Ashley frowned, then said, "Well, I resent the implication that my mother could have possibly had anything to do with this mess."

"I'm just looking for the truth. I know you all came in different cars. Why was that?"

"It just seemed easier that way."

"I suppose that's true," he said.

"And what do you mean by that? Alex, I don't like the way this conversation is going, and I won't sit here while you question me about my family."

Alex said, "Wait a second," but she was already gone. Vernum still trimmed, oblivious to what had happened. The man truly was in his own little world when he was working with his tools.

Elise quietly joined him from the corner of the building

where she'd been standing out of sight, listening. "Well, that went well."

"I made a mess of it, didn't I," Alex confessed.

"Don't be so sure," Elise said. "You didn't say anything all that bad. Ashley definitely overreacted. She's rattled about something."

"About what, I wonder?"

Elise said, "Alex, all you can do is stir things up and see what happens. You can bet she'll tell Cynthia about your conversation the second she and Steven get back to the inn. So where do we go from here?"

"I think we should go ahead and talk to Julie," Alex said. "If the will was never modified after Mathias's letter of intent to her, she'd have a huge motive to make sure that particular document never saw the light of day."

"So what are we waiting for?" Elise asked as she headed for Alex's truck.

As they drove to Amy's, Elise asked, "So who are your main suspects now?"

It was a game they'd played before, laying out their thoughts as they drove somewhere in Alex's truck.

After a moment of thought, Alex said, "Cynthia's got to be near the top, but Steven and Ashley aren't far behind. Julie could be guilty; I'm not as willing to count her out until we find out a little more information." Alex drove a minute, then added, "I hate to even mention it, but I guess there's still a chance that Tony's lying and I'm wrong about him after all. But I don't believe it." Alex gripped the steering wheel harder. Were his mixed feelings about his brother tainting his logic, causing him to overcompensate for the battles they'd had in the past?

Elise said, "Alex, you don't even need to consider that possibility at the moment. Leave that avenue to Sheriff

Armstrong. The best thing you can do for Tony is to focus on the people Sheriff Armstrong isn't looking at."

"Yeah, I know you're right," Alex said as he drove. He tapped the steering wheel. "Anybody else we should add to the list of suspects?"

"None that I can think of." Elise looked out the window as she added, "How about Sandra? Could she be wiping out her competition?"

Alex said, "Come on, I'm serious, Elise."

"Sorry, I shouldn't joke about that. I might as well accuse Vernum of the murder."

"If shears had been used, or maybe even a tree saw, but honestly, I doubt the man could stand being that close to anyone long enough to kill them."

Elise said, "There's one other suspect you haven't considered. Alex, is it possible Nadine killed your uncle?"

"My grade school teacher? Come on, Elise, what motive could she possibly have?"

Elise said, "What if she was stealing from Jase and he caught her? Could she have killed him in a panic and taken the files to throw the sheriff off her trail?"

Alex shook his head. "I'd trust that woman with my life. No, that's a stretch I can't make." Alex looked down the road as they neared Amy's studio and asked, "Elise, what's that?"

She looked ahead as he pointed to the sky, where a billowing mushroom cloud of smoke had suddenly exploded into the air.

Elise said, "Oh, no, it's not the inn again, is it, Alex?"

He shook his head. "No, it's in the wrong direction. I'm afraid it's Amy's place." Alex pushed his old truck harder, forcing it over the ruts of Amy's road. By the time they got closer to the house and barn-studio, they were assaulted by

burning odors, as well as waves of dancing ashes floating
in the air.

Amy's barn was on fire.

Without a second thought, Alex stopped the truck well
away from the burning barn and raced toward it on foot.

Elise yelled, "Do you think anyone's inside?" over the
roaring of the flames.

Alex pointed to the door. "If they are, they're trapped in
there. Elise, I'm going in." There was a long, wooden pin
jammed firmly into the hasp, securely locking the barn
door. Alex couldn't free it no matter how hard he tried, so
he ran around the barn, searching for some way in.

There was no other way in or out. The rear door had been
sealed ages ago, and the sole bank of windows were en-
gulfed in flames. Alex was back at the front, trying to figure a way to get inside, when he heard the pounding.
Someone was trying to get out!

Alex fought the pin with everything he had, but it was no
use; it was wedged firmly in place, as if someone had driven it in with a hammer. Looking around frantically on the
ground for something to use as a pry tool, Elise saw what
he was doing and retrieved the handle of the truck jack.
"Try this," she said, coughing from the smoke.

Alex took the steel rod and in less than a minute, he had
the hasp completely off. As the barn door swung open, the
fire inside exploded with the extra oxygen. Two figures lay
against a nearby wall covered with wet blankets. Alex
thought he might be too late until he saw one of the blankets move.

At least one of them was still alive!

He jumped through the flames licking at the opening and
was relieved to see that the fire hadn't spread everywhere
yet. Pulling at the blankets, Alex saw Amy's jet-black hair
peek out. "Come on, let's get out of here."

"I'm not leaving Julie," Amy said, her voice raspy from the smoke.

"I'll carry her. Can you walk?"

"I can make it, but I'm going to help you."

Alex screamed, "You need to get out! Now!" as the top of the barn exploded with flames and heat. The roar of the fire was unbelievable! Alex figured the barn couldn't stand very much longer under the assault, and he could feel the heat slapping at his skin as he struggled with Julie's unconscious body.

Somehow Alex managed to drag her to her feet, then he threw her over his shoulder. As quickly as he could, Alex raced toward his last hope of getting out alive.

As he took his third step out of the barn, the roof collapsed, sending shooting sparks at his heels as he ran for safety with Julie draped across his back.

Once he was well clear of the fire, he put Julie down. Amy, lying nearby, screamed, "How is she?"

I don't know yet," Alex answered as he tried to find a pulse. Julie hadn't been burned, that was something, but Alex knew that a great many people who died in fires expired from smoke inhalation, not the fire itself.

Elise said, "Move over, Alex," as she gently nudged him out of the way. She bent over Julie, then started administering CPR.

Alex heard a fire truck in the distance, then an ambulance siren close behind. He saw that Elise was doing everything for Julie that could be done, so he approached Amy.

Through a coughing spell, she asked, "How's Julie? Is she going to be all right?"

"Elise is doing all she can. What happened in there, Amy?"

She shook her head. "I don't know. I was showing Julie

how to weld, and the next second, it was dark. The barn door slammed shut. I thought it was a joke at first, then I smelled smoke. The whole side of the barn went up at once, and we were blocked off from the windows. I always keep a bucket of water around when I'm welding, so I soaked a few tarps in it and covered us up. It was the only thing I could think to do."

"You did great," Alex said as the ambulance pulled up first. Two EMTs jumped out and headed toward them. Alex said, "She needs your help first," as he pointed to Julie and Elise.

One of the paramedics said, "What about her?" as he gestured to Amy.

"I'm fine," Amy yelled. "Help her!"

The fire truck rolled up a few seconds later, with Mor and a dozen other volunteer firefighters from Elkton Falls on board. Chief Weston, the small wiry man who crewed the staff, took one look at the blaze, then asked Alex, "Anyone else inside?"

Amy shook her head. "We're both out."

Weston said, "Thank heaven for small favors. Okay men, let's hose down the perimeter and keep that fire from the house."

Amy tried to stand, and Alex had to help her climb to her feet. "You're not going to try to save my studio?"

Alex looked at the inferno and watched as the chief tried to explain. "Ma'am, it's too far gone. I can't afford to risk any of my men when there's no one inside. I'm sorry."

"But my life is in there," Amy cried. She tried to run to the flames, but Alex held her tightly in his arms.

"Amy, it's gone."

"It's just not fair," Amy cried as she melted into Alex's arms. "Who would do such an awful thing?"

That was something Alex wanted to know himself. He looked over to see the EMTs load Julie into the ambulance, strapped firmly to a gurney.

As they started to close the doors, Amy said, "Wait. I'm going with you."

"Sorry, there's no room," one of the techs said.

Amy said, "Then make room, I'm coming along," as she forced her way aboard.

Alex said, "She was in the fire, too. You've got to take her with you." There wasn't time to argue, and Amy's singed presence surely added to the urgency of her demand, so the attendants acquiesced.

After they pulled out, Elise joined Alex. They watched the barn burn in on itself, the flames leveling everything within reach. Alex looked over at Elise and saw tears tracking down the soot on her face. For the first time since he'd known her, there was no light in her eyes.

"What is it?" Alex asked her gently.

Elise could barely mumble out her next words, "Alex, I didn't get any response the entire time I worked on her. I don't think she's going to make it."

18

Alex put an arm around her. "Elise, you were the only chance she had, and you did the very best you could. The rescue squad was still working on her when they pulled out. There's still hope."

Elise whimpered, "Oh Alex, what I did just wasn't good enough. I know it."

Alex wrapped her in his arms, and she started to cry. In all the times he dreamed of holding her, he never thought it would be because of anything like what had just happened.

After a few minutes, Elise pulled back. "You smell like smoke," she said as she crinkled her nose.

"I know. Are you okay?"

She wiped a few errant tears from her cheek. "I will be now. Thanks, Alex."

"No thanks necessary. If you'll wait for me in the truck, I'll just be a minute. I need to talk to the chief."

"Take your time. I'll be okay now."

Alex walked over to Chief Weston and said, "I thought you should know, it was arson. Amy said someone slammed the barn door, then torched the place with them inside."

"I don't suppose she got a look at who did it, did she?"

Alex shook his head. "They were working on something inside and were distracted."

Mor trotted up to them, his face smudged from the fire. He was holding a scorched gas can gingerly by its handle. "They didn't even try to hide it. We found this right out in the open."

Weston said, "Leave it for the fire marshal; this is a case for him."

Mor nodded. "How are the women, Alex?"

"Julie was still unconscious when the ambulance left. I think Amy's going to be all right."

Mor asked, "How's Elise doing?"

Alex said, "She was a little shaken up, but both women would be dead if she hadn't done some quick thinking."

Weston said, "I understand you get some of the credit yourself. Amy said you were the one who carried Julie out of the burning building."

"Anybody would have done the same thing if they'd been here," Alex said.

Weston replied, "Don't be so sure. You did good, Alex."

"Let's just hope she makes it."

Weston nodded his agreement, and Alex asked, "Can you let me know what happens here after the fire marshal leaves?"

"I'd say you're an interested party. Sure, I'll give you a call."

Alex joined Elise in the truck.

"What did they say?" she asked.

"They agree that it's arson, but nobody has the slightest idea who did it."

"No one but us," Elise said.

Alex nodded. "So you think it was one of our suspects? I guess Ashley's off the hook, anyway."

"Alex, she could have run over here and set the fire before we could drive the distance in your truck. You said yourself how close the two places really are. I'm afraid she's still on the list."

Alex sighed. "So we're right back where we started."

Elise said, "I wouldn't say that. There's one thing we know for sure. Tony didn't have anything to do with the fire. Even Armstrong should be able to see that."

"You've got a point, but I'm not sure Armstrong will believe the fire is related to Jase's murder."

As they neared the inn, Elise said, "So what do we do now?"

"Tell you what. After we get cleaned up, why don't you talk to Steven, and I'll focus on Cynthia. If we can split them up, maybe we'll be able to get more out of them."

"Cynthia, can you spare a minute?" After Alex and Elise had taken showers and changed, they had spotted Cynthia and Steven in the lobby, sharing a whispered conversation. Elise had agreed to hang back while Alex got Cynthia's attention before taking her turn with Steven.

"I'm busy at the moment," Cynthia snapped.

"Whenever you get the chance then," Alex said as he drifted back to the reservation desk.

Cynthia said, "Are you going to just hover there until we're finished?"

Alex said, "Sorry," then moved into his office. Elise joined him a few minutes later. She said, "You're not going to believe this. Cynthia just ordered me out of the lobby when she saw me waiting for you."

"She threw me out, too, and I own the place. What do you think is going on out there?"

"I wish I knew. I can't stop thinking about Julie. I wonder how she's doing?"

Alex pointed to the telephone. "Why don't you call the hospital and find out? I'd like to know myself."

Elise scooted the phone over to him. "Would you do it?"

Alex nodded, then looked up the number and dialed. After a brief conversation with the information desk, he hung up and said, "She's in serious but stable condition, that's all they'd tell me."

Elise said with a sigh, "At least she's still alive. That's something. I've got an idea how we might find out more about what's going on over there."

Elise took the phone and hit Redial, then asked for Amy to be paged. After a moment, she asked again, then had a brief conversation with the sculptor. The look of relief on Elise's face was apparent.

After she hung up, Elise said, "Amy just talked to the doctor. It looks like Julie's going to be all right."

"Thanks to you," Alex said.

"I seem to remember somebody else there, too."

Alex nodded. "Okay, we both did good. I'm just glad we came along when we did. Let's not mention the fire to the Trasks yet. We might be able to use it."

Without warning, Cynthia Shays-Trask burst into Alex's office. "What's this I hear about your brother being arrested for the attorney's murder? Did he say what he did with the will? I still don't understand why he took it in the first place, but we would greatly appreciate it if he would return the document to us."

Alex said, "I'm sorry, but you're mistaken. Tony didn't kill Jase."

Cynthia eyed him narrowly. "But he *is* currently in jail for the crime, isn't he?"

Elise said calmly, "He's being questioned by the police, but we're certain he's innocent."

Cynthia patted Elise's arm. "Of course you are, dear." She turned to Alex. "If it turns out to be otherwise, I meant what I said." She looked at Alex a moment, then added, "Now, what was it you wanted to talk to me about?"

Elise took her cue beautifully. "If you'll excuse me, I have work to do," she said as she escaped, no doubt off in search of Steven.

Alex gestured to the empty chair. "Please, sit down."

Cynthia said, "This won't take long, will it? I need to speak further with my son."

"Is there something wrong?" Alex asked.

"That faux daughter is not going to steal my children's inheritance. We're working out our strategy to stop her, and I think we've come up with something."

Alex blurted out, "Don't you even care that she's in the hospital?" So much for keeping that information a secret.

Cynthia's gaze hardened. She fought to hide the surprise on her face, but the mask slipped for just a moment. She was hearing about the accident for the first time, as far as Alex could tell. "What are you talking about?"

"There was a fire at the place she was staying. She was nearly killed."

Cynthia stood. "But she survived."

With some satisfaction, Alex said, "The doctors say she's going to be fine. Let me ask you something. Have you considered the possibility that Julie really is Mathias's daughter, that she deserves to be included in the inheritance?"

"My husband was many things, Alex, but even he wasn't scoundrel enough to pop this on us without warning. I wouldn't believe a DNA test at this point. There's something suspicious about this entire scenario."

She started to leave as Alex asked, "What do you think was in the stolen will?"

"How should I know? My husband was famous for his erratic behavior his entire life. The 'sound body and mind' clause is enough to have the entire document disputed, even if the will is found. One thing you may bank on: my children will be provided for; I'll make sure of that." Cynthia hesitated at the door, lost in her own thoughts. After a few moments of silence, she added, "We won't make any agreements with this usurper. My children will not be denied what is rightfully theirs."

After Cynthia was gone, Alex stared at the door after her departure. The woman was single-minded about protecting what she thought of as rightly hers and her children's. He couldn't help wondering if she would go so far as to try to use a match and a can of gasoline to settle the dispute once and for all.

Elise came in a few minutes later. "Well, that was useless. Steven would barely talk to me. I could hardly get a word out of him when his mother stormed out, accusing me of browbeating her son. I hope you managed better than I did."

Alex said, "I'm not sure." He shared Cynthia's comments and his theory that she might have taken matters into her own hands.

"Alex, I have a hard time believing she would go that far. We don't even know how much money Mathias left behind. How can we possibly know if it was enough to kill for?"

Alex leaned back in his chair. "I don't think it matters all that much to Cynthia. I believe she considers it a matter of principle."

"So where does that leave us in our investigation?"

Alex stood. "There's nothing we can do here at the moment. Why don't we head over to the hospital and see if Julie saw something Amy might have missed. I particularly want to ask her if she remembers hearing a car pull up, or if the arsonist was on foot."

"Let's go," Elise said.

"Aren't you worried about our guests?" Alex said with a smile.

"They can take care of themselves," she said.

•　•　•

They found Amy stationed just outside Julie's room. Someone had cleaned her face and tended to the cuts on her hands where she'd tried to break out of the barn, but she hadn't changed clothes yet.

Elise said, "Amy, I didn't even think about what you'd wear. Can I run back to your house and get you something to change into?"

"It's kind of you to offer, but I'm fine."

Alex asked, "Any news about Julie?"

"The doctor's in with her now. Armstrong came by ten minutes ago. He wanted to know if we heard or saw anything unusual before the fire."

"And did you?" Alex asked.

"No, neither one of us had anything to tell him. It just kind of happened, do you know what I mean? I was caught completely off guard."

"I can only imagine how frightening it must have been for you two in that barn," Elise said.

Amy sighed, still hoarse from the smoke she'd inhaled. "Do you want to know the truth? All I could think about was that it was all my fault."

Alex asked, "How can that possibly be true?"

"I knew Julie was in danger. I should have been taking more precautions than I did to protect her."

Alex asked, "What are you talking about?"

"Come on, it sounds like there is a ton of money at stake here, and people go crazy sometimes when that much temptation is involved. What was I thinking, trying to protect her all alone? I'll never forgive myself for what happened."

Elise leaned over her and hugged Amy. "How could you possibly know that some maniac would come after her? Amy, you saved both your lives today, you know that, don't you? If you hadn't covered yourselves with those soaked tarps, you'd both be dead."

Amy said, "What if it wasn't enough? She's not completely out of danger yet."

The door opened, and a doctor in a white lab coat stepped out. He approached them and said, "Amy, are you all right?"

"I'm fine, Doctor. How is she?"

"Better, actually. I increased her medication, and she's sleeping now."

"When can we see her?" Alex asked.

"She's not up for visitors," the doctor said. "Until and unless her family arrives, I'm restricting her visitors to Amy at the moment." He turned back to the sculptor and added, "You can go back in, but don't wake her. She needs her sleep."

"I won't say a word," Amy said as she slipped back inside.

Alex said, "How's she really doing?"

"May I ask your connection with the patient?"

Elise said stiffly, "He pulled her out of the burning barn. Doesn't that give him the right to some answers?"

The doctor nodded, a slight smile spreading on his face. "Not officially, but it certainly does in my book. I didn't know. I believe Ms. Hart should recover completely, given that she's young and strong." He turned back to Elise. "Amy told me about you as well. Her description was flawless. I'm assuming you were the one who administered CPR."

"I did," she said simply.

"Nicely done. You saved her life today, there's no doubt in my mind."

As the doctor walked away, Alex saw movement down the corridor in the other direction. A masked male doctor was hurrying away from them, and Alex wouldn't have thought a thing out of the ordinary if he hadn't noticed the man's shoes.

They were thick-soled boots, not the shoes he'd expect from a doctor on duty at all.

Alex rushed down the corridor, but by the time he turned the corner, whoever had been there was gone.

•   •   •

"What was that all about?" Elise asked as she caught up to him.

"It's not important," Alex answered. "My imagination must be on overtime."

Elise said, "So where do we go from here?"

Alex thought about it a moment, then said, "I think it's time we head back to the inn. I've got the germ of an idea on how to get the real killer out into the open."

"What do you have in mind?"

"If I tell you now, you'll just try to talk me out of it," Alex said with a slight smile.

"So it's dangerous. Are you going to at least tell Sheriff Armstrong what you're up to?"

"He'd just try to stop me, too."

Elise looked at him solemnly. "If I promise not to interfere, would you tell me then?"

Alex thought about it a moment, then said with a grin, "Tell you what. Maybe you can even help, if you're interested."

"Count me in."

19

As they drove back to Hatteras West, Alex explained his plan to Elise. "I'm going to spend some time going through the boxes from Jase's office. At just the right moment, I'm going to find a copy of Mathias's will."

Elise protested, "But how can you do that? Cynthia's going to demand to see it."

Alex said, "I'll pretend to call Sandra, then lock it up somewhere I can keep my eye on it. Then we'll see who comes after it."

"It sounds dangerous to me, Alex."

"What choice do I have? Armstrong's not going to let Tony out, he doesn't believe the arson and murder are related, based on the phone conversation we had earlier. I know better than anybody else how strong the evidence is against my brother. That anonymous caller really got to him."

"Alex, you believe me when I say it wasn't me, don't you?"

He risked a quick glance at her. "Of course I do. I just wish I knew how Armstrong got the information."

"You should try calling Nadine again."

Alex said, "You know I won't carry a cellular phone; I don't want to be accessible all the time. It can wait till we get back to the inn."

He swung the truck up Point Road and saw the parking lot in front of the inn sported all the cars in question. "Looks like everybody's here. Are you ready?"

"I'm still not sure about it, but I'll do all I can to make it work."

He patted her shoulder. "Don't worry. It's going to be fine."

After they were inside, Alex checked the answering machine and saw he had one message. It was Mor. "Alex, we need to talk. Fighting that fire really brought things to a head for me. I've made my decision."

When Alex tried to call his friend back at Mor or Les, there was no answer at the handyman's shop. Instead of playing telephone tag and leaving a message, Alex hung up. His friend would just have to wait.

The lobby was empty, so Alex made sure his door was open as he and Elise started going through boxes. Elise said softly, "Do you really think they're going to buy this?"

"It's the only thing left I can do," Alex said. "We just have to wait a little longer, then we'll be able to start the show."

Alex and Elise kept digging through the boxes of books. At first, Alex thought he might have actually found a single copy of the will serving double duty as a bookmark, but it turned out to be a detailed letter from one of Jase's clients firing him. There was the oddest collection of documents Jase used to mark his place from whatever was handy. It was a glimpse inside his uncle's life as he moved from book to book, more for the flotsam and jetsam than from the actual reading material. Alex took one legal-sized envelope and found a canceled Deed of Trust in it. The envelope itself was blank, so Alex scrawled something mimicking

Jase's handwriting on the front and showed it to Elise. "What do you think?"

"It either says, 'Last Will and Testament of Mathias Trask' or it's a party announcement for an eleven-year-old girl named Emily Hannah."

Alex smiled, "Good enough. We want to leave things as vague as we can."

Alex heard someone moving around on the porch, then the front door opened. Cynthia and Steven walked in, and Alex winked at Elise. "It's show time."

"Here it is!" he shouted. "I found it."

"Oh my goodness. What are you going to do?" Elise asked in a like voice.

"I've got to call Sandra. It's a legal document; she'll know what to do with it."

Alex pretended to dial the phone and watched as Cynthia hurried toward them. As she reached the door, he said into the dead telephone, "I found the will."

After a pause, he added, "Can't you come out and get it now?"

Cynthia said, "What's going on here?"

Alex held his hand up, then said, "I understand. I'll keep it safe out here and bring it to you in the morning. Thanks."

After he hung up, Cynthia spied the document in his hand. "What have you got there?"

"It's Mathias's will," he said proudly. "I found it in one of the boxes of Jase's things."

"Give it to me," she demanded as she tried to snatch the document out of his hands.

"I can't," Alex said, moving away from her. Cynthia's sharp nails clamped down on air, but just barely. "Alex Winston, you are an innkeeper, not an attorney. As a representative of my late husband's estate, that document belongs to me."

Alex shook his head. "As much as I'd like to oblige, Cynthia, Sandra instructed me to hold onto it until tomorrow, and since she's taken over Jase's cases officially, she's the executor of Mathias's will." Alex didn't know or care if he was technically right; it sounded good and would most likely be enough to satisfy Cynthia.

He was wrong.

"I'm calling my own attorney. I won't tolerate this for one moment. Do you understand me?"

Alex said, "Is the call long distance?"

"Of course it is. Do you think I would ever agree to use an attorney in this backward little town?"

Alex said, "Sorry, then, you'll have to use the telephone in your room. It's the only way I can bill it out properly."

Cynthia started to burn when Steven said, "You want privacy anyway, don't you, Mother? Why don't you walk out onto the porch? You can use my cell phone."

She agreed and stormed off outside after grabbing the telephone from her son's hand. Alex hoped the attorney was out of the office. He'd waited as long as he could, but there was a chance his plan would be thwarted before it had time to work. It would be embarrassing admitting that he'd lied, but if it helped save Tony, it would be worth it.

Steven drifted upstairs, no doubt to avoid his mother's foul mood, and after they were both gone, Elise said, "So what do we do now?"

He tapped the document with his finger. "There's nothing much we can do but wait."

Half an hour later, Steven and Ashley came downstairs together, with Ashley holding the urn full of their father's ashes. Cynthia had stormed upstairs long ago. Evidently, her lawyer was already gone for day, just as Alex had hoped. Steven was carrying the urn that held his father's ashes. "Alex, do you have a minute?"

"I'm sorry, Steven, but I can't give you the will any more

than I can turn it over to your mother. Sandra's instructions were firm."

"That's not it at all," Ashley said. "Steven and I were so impressed with the ceremony scattering your uncle's ashes that we wondered if we could do the same with our father."

"I don't know if I'm up to another send-off, Ashley, and I know the town council won't approve a lighting so close to last night."

Steven said, "We don't want any of that. We just wanted to make sure it was okay with you if we did it ourselves at the top of the lighthouse, just the two of us."

Elise said, "Don't you want to ask your mother to join you?"

"No, she doesn't have a sentimental bone in her body," Ashley said. "Steven and I want to do this together."

Alex looked at them intently, then said, "Let me ask you this. If Julie's truly his daughter, too, doesn't she have a right to be there as well?"

Ashley said, "Steven and I grew up with him. She knows him through a single letter. Even if they share DNA, he's still not her father. Please."

Elise said, "She's got a point, Alex."

"Go ahead then," Alex said. "Put this sign up when you go in. Everyone around here will respect it." Alex dug through a drawer and pulled out a Lighthouse Closed sign.

"Thanks, we greatly appreciate it," Ashley said as an errant tear ran down her cheek.

"Are you all right?" Elise asked her.

"Excuse me," Ashley said as she hurried out of the room.

Steven lingered behind. "Ashley's been really feeling Dad's absence lately. This is all too much for her."

"Funny, she said the same thing about you, Steven," Alex said.

"Sure, I was upset, but she was his favorite, no matter what she says. I'd better get up there. She shouldn't be alone."

After Steven was gone, Elise said, "So, where's your safekeeping spot?"

Alex moved over to his bed and pulled out one of Jase's books on hidden treasures from beneath it. It was the volume he'd taken from his uncle's desk in his office. "It's kind of appropriate we use this as a bookmark, don't you think?"

As Alex opened the book to put the document inside, a single sheet of stationery fluttered out. Alex retrieved it, and as he read, his face went white.

"What is it?" Elise asked as Alex bolted for the door.

"Call Armstrong, Elise. I know who killed Jase, and if I don't act fast enough, somebody else is going to die."

Alex heard voices above him as he raced up the lighthouse stairs. He had to get to the top before something happened! For one of the few times in his life, he cursed every one of the 268 stairs that led to the top of the lighthouse. As he raced upward, Alex's heart pounded in his chest. Would he get there in time, or would another victim be taken at the top of the lighthouse he so loved?

No, he couldn't let that happen.

Not again.

20

"Go ahead, Ashley, pour the ashes out over the edge."

"Steven, you should help me, too."

"Okay, I'm coming," Steven said as Alex burst through the door.

Ashley saw him and said, "We'd really rather be alone right now, if you don't mind."

"Yes, Alex, this is a private ceremony," Steven said in a hard voice. Alex saw he was two steps from his sister as he said it.

"That's close enough," Alex said. "Ashley, move away from the railing."

Steven saw the look on Alex's face and knew instantly he'd been discovered. Taking a bold step, he moved toward his sister, pinning her against the narrow railing.

"Steven! What are you doing?"

"Shut up, Sister dear. You're going to have a little accident up here."

"Have you lost your mind?" Ashley yelled.

Steven put more pressure on her, and Alex could see

Ashley beginning to go over. There was no safety net below, and if she went off the side, it was a 200-foot drop.

"Are you going to push us both over, Steven?" Alex said, stalling for time.

"That's exactly what I'm going to do. You're going to fall trying to save her. Sadly, I couldn't get to you in time," Steven said. "Congratulations, Alex, you're going to die a hero."

"Why are you doing this?" Ashley cried.

"Stop your whimpering," Steven said. "Good old Alex finally found the will, so as soon as I take care of you both, I'm going to go to his room and destroy it. I just happen to know where Dad's old will is. Mother keeps a copy in her desk at home. She thinks it's useless, can you believe that? I slipped a look at it, and guess what? If either of us dies before the will's read, that share is gone, whether we have children of our own or not. I tried to take care of Julie before it became an issue, but she'll just have to wait. I have to kill you now, Ashley, before the old will is legally entered into the record."

Alex, trying to stall until Armstrong could arrive, said, "Was your mother in on this as well? Did she help you try to kill Amy and Julie?"

"Mother?" Steven laughed. "She doesn't have it in her. I ditched her in town and drove back to that barn by myself. If you hadn't stumbled along, it would have worked perfectly, too. Oh well, half the pie is better than a third, as soon as I take care of my newly discovered sister. She's going to suffer from complications tonight, whether she knows it or not." He grinned slightly, then added, "As to the rest of Father's fortune, after today, I'll be Mother's only beneficiary. Who knows what might happen to her then."

Alex said desperately, "Steven, I didn't find a copy of the new will. I was just bluffing." Alex paused a moment, then added, "I did find the letter you wrote Jase, though. That's what you were looking for when you snatched the envelope, wasn't it? He must have stuffed it in the book on his desk just before he died. You had to have had a good reason to believe that your father had written you out of his will going in. Why?"

"Somehow he found out about my gambling all the way down in South America. I got a postcard three weeks before he died telling me that I was no longer his son, if you can believe that. I wrote to Jase, since he drafted the earlier will, to see if it was true, but he called me, dismissed my questions, and wouldn't tell me a thing. That's when I decided to visit him in his office and put a little extra pressure on him. He flaunted my letter at me, or at least the envelope I'd sent it in. I reached for it, even had two fingers on it, but the old man hit me with a book, can you believe it? By the time I got off the ground, the letter was gone. All I found was the envelope. The crafty old buzzard hid it in plain sight."

"Is that why you killed him? Did you push Jase too far?"

"He started for the safe, and I knew in my heart the will had to be there. The second Jase opened it, I tapped him on the back of the head with that lighthouse paperweight. I wasn't trying to kill him, but I guess his old skull was a little too fragile. And then I couldn't find the blasted thing! The folder was empty," Steven protested, easing up on his grip on Ashley. "You're bluffing, Alex. You really found it, didn't you? Lying now isn't going to do you any good."

Alex heard a foot scraping on the edge of the top stair, and he hoped it was Armstrong. Instead, out of the corner of his eye he saw that it was Vernum!

And Alex suddenly knew why he was there.

He said, "That's the thing, Steven. I'm willing to bet that folder was always empty. There wasn't any need for a new will at all. It just wasn't an issue. Come on out, Vernum, this concerns you. Or should I call you Mathias?"

• • •

Alex held his breath, wondering if his leap of deduction
was correct. Too many things had added up for him to deny
it.

One look at Vernum's face told Alex that he'd guessed
correctly.

"Did Jase tell you?" was all Mathias could say.

Alex said, "No, he'd never violate a trust. It's the only
way things added up. Whenever I spotted you on the
grounds, you were near where your family was, even if it
meant you had to be around other people to be close to
them. I found you trimming shrubs you'd already tackled
the day they arrived, remember? It was out of character,
and it made me suspicious. Then, on the porch, I swear you
were getting ready to tell me something when Ashley came
out. You admitted knowing Jase, and I couldn't see your
paths crossing in that many ways until I realized that you'd
need an old friend to help pull this off, and I could easily
see it appealing to my uncle's off beat sense of humor.
Then when I found an odd-looking stamp in the shed where
you were sleeping, I remembered Ashley talking about your
stamp collection on the day she arrived. As soon as I put it
all together, it was the only way your behavior made
sense."

Ashley said, "This can't be true. Our father is dead."

Steven said, "Nice try, Alex, but I'm not buying it either.
He's not Mathias Trask."

Vernum said wearily, "I suspected you'd doubt me. You
both need proof? Steven, when you were nine you had a
crush on Lilly Taylor. You sold your bicycle to a friend in
order to buy her flowers, remember? And Ashley, when you
were seven you scraped your knee on a fence rail. Remember how you cried in my lap? I gave you one of my rings to
cheer you up, and you asked me if you broke your arm
would you get a new car, remember?"

Ashley said, "But you were so fat! And your hair! Nothing's the same about you."

In a deep, rich tone, Vernum said, "Nothing? Don't you recognize my voice? I have changed rather dramatically, haven't I? I don't miss carrying around all that extra weight, but I must admit, I'm looking forward to being clean-shaven again."

Ashley was ready to believe, but Steven couldn't. "So Cynthia told you all that family history. So what?"

"Son, it's true. There's no reason to hurt your sister. I'm sorry to say that there is no great estate waiting for you on the other end. Truth be told, I'm nearly broke. All I have left are my stamps and my family."

Steven shoved Ashley toward them, but before Alex could tackle him, he pulled out a gun. Ashley stumbled into Alex, the urn suddenly in Alex's hands.

Alex asked, "Who am I holding, Mathias?"

"Ashes from my grill, Alex. Son, give it up. There's no escape for you, can't you see that?"

Steven said, "That's where you're wrong. Nobody had better get in my way. I'm getting out of here."

Vernum said, "You're not going anywhere, Son."

"You think I won't shoot you?" Steven screamed as he turned the gun toward his own father.

Alex seized the chance and threw the urn's contents into Steven's face. The ashes blinded him for a moment, and Alex dove for the hand holding the gun. One shot fired as they wrestled for it, and Alex suddenly felt himself heading over the rail!

With a final lunge, Alex grasped the rail as he was going over! As he held on with all his might, Steven pounded at his hands, fighting to break his grip. As Alex looked on helplessly, Vernum pulled Steven away. He could hear them scuffling, but he couldn't spare a second's concentration. Suddenly, Alex heard a shot. If Steven had retrieved the pistol, Alex knew that the next bullet was for him. Fighting to pull himself back up over the edge, he could feel the railing slip in his grasp.

Then Ashley's hands reached over and helped steady him as he somehow managed to climb back to safety.

As Alex slumped against the rail, he looked over to see Steven lying near his feet, a small pool of blood forming around him. Vernum held his son's head in his arms, crying softly. Ashley joined him, and the two of them held their own private wake over the body.

Elise rushed through the door, with Armstrong a few steps behind. She threw herself on Alex, smothering him with her embrace. "Oh, Alex, when I saw you go over the rail, I nearly died. I can't believe you're all right."

"Take it easy. I'm still a little shaky."

As she helped him up, Armstrong said, "What happened here?"

"Steven killed Jase trying to get a will that was never written. He tried to kill Ashley, then he went after me a few minutes ago. That's all I know," Alex said.

Vernum looked at the sheriff, then said, "My real name is Mathias Trask. My son killed himself when he realized he couldn't get away with it any longer. I tried to stop him, but I wasn't fast enough. Isn't that right, Ashley?"

She looked at her father a full beat before she said, "That's exactly the way it happened, Father."

Suicide? Alex had heard them struggling. It was most likely self-defense, but Alex was almost positive that if Vernum's hands were tested for gunpowder, the truth would come out. And who would it serve? Steven had killed Jase; Alex had heard the confession himself. Was it possible Vernum was telling the truth? Or was he lying to himself already, trying to create a memory he could live with that didn't put his own finger anywhere near the trigger? Either way, Alex would never know what had really happened while he'd been fighting for his life.

Cynthia joined them, nearly out of breath. She saw Steven lying there, then began to wail. "Get away from my son!" she shouted at Vernum.

"Cyn, it's me. He's my son, too."

Cynthia threw herself at Vernum. "You killed him! You killed him, Mathias." All it took was the sound of his voice for her to know her husband. So that was why Vernum always ran whenever someone else was near. He'd only talk to people who hadn't known him before, for fear of giving himself away.

Mathias let his wife pound on him, taking it all without flinching. Cynthia cried, "You did this with your stupid little game. You might as well have pulled the trigger yourself."

Mathias said, "I just wanted to see my family again, and I wanted you all to get to know Julie. Nothing else mattered. I'm so sorry. I never dreamed it would end like this."

Cynthia collapsed, and Armstrong was right behind her. "Ma'am, let me help you down the steps. You don't need to be here."

Cynthia turned to look at the body of her son one last time, then stumbled away with the sheriff. Mathias turned to Ashley. "You believe my intent, don't you?"

"I've missed you so much," Ashley said as the two of them followed the rest down, never answering his question.

Alex took Elise's hand and said, "Let's go."

Elise said, "I'm so sorry this all happened up here, Alex."

He shook his head. "The lighthouse takes it all in, the good and bad. We spread Jase's ashes up here, and his killer died less than a foot away from that exact spot. There's a kind of justice to it all."

Cynthia left to make arrangements in town for Steven, while Mathias and Ashley caught up on their lives with the sheriff hovering nearby. Alex was surprised to find Tony waiting for him at the bottom of the lighthouse steps, his luggage at his feet. Alex and Elise had descended slowly, his legs still shaky from nearly going over the edge.

"So you're out of jail," Alex said gladly.

"Armstrong was just letting me go when Elise called. I came out to make sure you were okay."

"Tony, why don't you hang around?" Alex asked. "We could get to know one another again."

Tony shook his head. "Thanks, but I'm done with family reunions. All this place has left for me is bad memories."

"I'm sorry you feel that way," Alex said.

"Don't be; it's not your fault. Vernum told me *he* was the source of the anonymous phone call. He heard you and Elise talking at Bear Rocks and jumped to his own conclusion. Turns out he and Jase were friends from way back, and he truly thought I'd killed him."

"Don't leave it like this," Alex pleaded.

Tony said, "It's the only way it can be." He offered a hand to Alex, and despite everything, despite the pain and hard feelings they'd shared over the years, Alex stepped inside the extended hand and hugged his brother. He knew in his heart it was probably the last time he'd ever see Tony, and he didn't want to end it with just a handshake.

His brother was obviously surprised by the hug, but he didn't fight Alex's embrace. After a few moments, he pulled away. "Good-bye, Alex."

"Good-bye, Tony. You know you're always welcome here."

Tony looked around one last time. "It's not home for me anymore, Alex."

And then he drove away, without a single look back.

21

The inn was nearly empty again, at least for the moment.
Ashley left to find her mother with Mathias by her side.
There was an uneasy truce between Mathias and Cynthia,
and Alex wondered how it would all work out. He'd heard
the older man trying to talk Ashley into visiting Julie at the
hospital, but he wasn't having much success. Tony's room
was empty, and they didn't have any more guests scheduled
until the weekend.

Alex had just finished paying the last of a stack of bills
when Mor walked in.

"Got a second?" his friend asked.

"I've been meaning to return your call, but things were a
little tense around here."

"So I heard," Mor said.

"You said you've made up your mind. I'm going to miss
you, Mor. You've been like a brother to me."

Mor continued his frown, but he couldn't hold back any
longer, and a smile exploded. "You're not getting rid of me

that easily. I've decided to hang around Elkton Falls. Who else is going to keep you out of trouble?"

Alex couldn't believe the good news. "What made you change your mind?"

"Les and his lady friend had a parting of the ways. He never wanted to retire; she was pushing him into it so she could help him spend his money. You know how tight he is! Can you imagine him forking over his money for cruises and minks? He had a fit. No, it's back to business as usual for Mor or Les."

Alex hugged his friend. "I'm really glad you're staying."

Mor hugged him back, then pulled away. "Hey, don't get mushy on me here. Well, I'd better get back to work. I've been slacking off lately, and I've got a backlog of calls you wouldn't believe. I want to get caught up before Emma gets into town. See you around, Alex."

"Bye, Mor. And welcome back."

"Hey buddy, I was never gone," he said as he walked out, smiling.

Alex missed Jase, but the rest of his world was back the way he liked it. Tony had been right; Hatteras West was his home, and his complete world.

Elise knocked on the door soon after Mor left and said, "Alex, we need to talk."

Oh, well. Things had been great for a few minutes, anyway.

"Peter's not buying the cottage after all. He's moving back to West Virginia."

Alex steeled himself for the rest of the news. "And you're going back with him, aren't you?"

Elise looked startled by the comment. "Is that what you want, Alex?"

"I want you to stay," he blurted out. "I thought you knew that."

"Of course I'm staying. Seeing you dangling off the edge of the lighthouse made me realize I belong here with you. The engagement is off." She paused a moment, then added, "Alex, would you like to take me out to dinner?"

"What, you mean like a date?"

Elise smiled. "Don't you think it's high time we had one?"

Alex returned her grin. "I'd say so. So, where are you taking me?"

"I thought we could go to Mamma Ravolini's. Irma's been bragging about a new dish I want to try."

"Were you asking me out for tonight? That's awfully short notice," Alex said with a grin.

"We don't have any guests, so why not? Tomorrow we'll have a nearly full house again. I can't wait until we open the rebuilt Dual Keepers' Quarters again."

Alex said, "For one night, let's not talk about Hatteras West."

"It's a deal," Elise said as she moved toward him.

About the Author

Tim Myers lives with his family near the Blue Ridge Mountains he loves and writes about. He is the award-winning author of the Agatha-nominated Lighthouse Inn mystery series as well as over seventy short stories.

Coming in October 2003, *At Wick's End* is the first in Tim's new Candlemaking mystery series, also from Berkley Prime Crime.

Tim has been a stay-at-home dad for the last eleven years, finding time for murder and mayhem whenever he can.

To learn more, visit his website at **www.timmyers.net** or contact him at **timothylmyers@hotmail.com**.